FAST
COMPANY

A Richard Jackson Book

FAST COMPANY

by D. James Smith

A DK INK BOOK
DK PUBLISHING, INC.

Grateful acknowledgment goes to my editor, Richard W. Jackson, for his warmth and wisdom; to my agent, Barbara Markowitz, for taking a chance on me; and to Valerie Hobbs for her generous encouragement. For their sharp eyes, special thanks to Annette, Josephine, Robin, Sonia, and Terry.

"Fern Hill" by Dylan Thomas, from *The Poems of Dylan Thomas.* Copyright © 1945 by the Trustees for The Copyrights of Dylan Thomas. Reprinted by permission of New Directions Publishing Corp. and David Higham Associates.

A Richard Jackson Book

DK Publishing, Inc.
95 Madison Avenue
New York, New York 10016

Visit us on the World Wide Web at http://www.dk.com

Cataloging-in-Publication data is available from the Library of Congress.

ISBN 0-7894-2625-0

Book design by Annemarie Redmond.
The text of this book is set in 11 point Janson Text.

Printed and bound in U.S.A.

First Edition, 1999
10 9 8 7 6 5 4 3 2 1

This book is dedicated to
Annette and Bill and Mike

In the sun that is young once only,
Time let me play and be
Golden in the mercy of his means . . .

—Dylan Thomas, "Fern Hill"

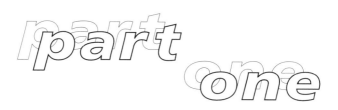

part one

1. Cat

Six times I saw Jason before he ever noticed me. I'm sure it was six because that was the year I had a lot of sixes occurring for me. In fact, I'd only had my period exactly six times the winter he spoke to me the first time. Six times I had opened the Bible at random, and always it was to a passage about sins of the flesh. There were six little welts that appeared mysteriously on my hand one day and six dreams in a row about dying.

I believed, then, that love was a kind of dying because I found that when it happened, I became someone strange and new. The gray streets, the old yellow leaves, even the moon, pink and heavy as a peach in the branches outside my window, looked new when love settled into my life, which had become, suddenly, something warm and sharp.

My twin died when I was small. My sister, Abigail. I could imagine her traveling, all those years, backward in some parallel world. Sometimes when I lay on my bed and stared at the ceiling and saw the world upside down, the light fixture standing up like an urn in the center of the room, I thought of her fluttering up there, and I felt tight in my heart, as if it were a fist, clenching and unclenching, and I could see how empty the room must've seemed to her up there with no furniture, and I hoped she took some satisfaction in what I was doing and how I

1

was trying to live with my whole self, true and without fear.

That was the year Jason and I got together, and so it was then that I learned he was afraid. I never told him because it's wrong to give people more than they can handle. Because he didn't want to be afraid. Because it wasn't his fault he was that way. And because love is the only good reason for *not* doing something.

First time I put on my skates, my blades, my *in-line* skates, I must've looked like a big ol' crow with my feet chained down. At least, that's what Cat's mom said. I kept stepping around in big circles, trying to keep from slamming the pavement and ruining my teeth. Later, of course, I *ruled* the streets. I had the whole package—elbow pads, knee guards, half gloves. Over on Jackson Street, where there's a hill, I could do 40 mph easy. Doug, Karendeep, Ozzie, and then Cat, sometimes in the evenings we traveled together, loud, fast. The Ravens, that was us.

You ever notice that friends have a way of becoming enemies? You hang with somebody long enough and the little things they do that you thought were what made them interesting at one time start to grate on you and then out of nowhere you might just walk over and clock them. You might not even be sure why you did it. But there it is. Now, I'm just the kind to do something like that—the unexpected.

You know, my dad liked to say I had issues. With anger. My dad was kind of irritating that way. Said stupid stuff like that. Read it in magazines somewhere and then thought he was on to something profound, and then I'd hear it for the rest of my life. It wouldn't have been so bad if he hadn't had the habit of talking to me very carefully and quietly as if I were mentally slow.

3

He had this big basset hound face with little flecks of pencil lead dropped in his big gray eyes and a watery voice that had a way of making me think of rain falling somewhere back in his head. I swear, when he talked to me, it was as if all the air in the room got damp; made me feel I'd a bad case of Hong Kong flu coming on. It was the worst if he'd had a few belts and was really warming up to the sound of his voice, brandy stinking up his wet little lips. Usually, I recommend you just settle in and nod at your folks when they get like that so they won't go and get helpless and pitiful on you.

"Bernard," my mother would say, "you talk to him." Mother was a sparrow—thin, little, flitting arms, thin neck, ol' brown wig on her head. Tired. I can't really imagine her ever having been a child, but I suppose she was one of those weak little kids you see sometimes that look like they were born too frail for this life. I'm sure that when she met my dad and his black brogues and his gray woolly trousers sagging in the butt and his big dog face, she knew right then her life was complete.

It took me thirteen, fourteen years to figure them out. You couldn't shock them. I burned down the garage once. They just crept around the house for a week treating me like I was a junior Charlie Manson. I think they were almost happy. They were sure I had BIG psychological problems. That's when Bernard invented that calm way of speaking to me.

One day I was sick and waited too long to ask Mrs. Callahan if I could go to the head, and I ended up barfing all over her big red geranium-print dress. They actually

4

thought I'd done it on purpose. Seriously, they were *that* out of it. I won't say that it wasn't interesting watching Callahan's face gettin' hot with horror, loud as her outfit. And the sorry little strangling sounds she made in the back of her throat were so fascinating that my whole class never really looked at her the same way again, but I did not vomit on an old lady for kicks. Would you?

You know, sometimes I'd watch a bird, maybe a seagull blown way inland by a storm, cruising overhead, and it would be, for a moment, like *I* was up there, the wind in my ears, the whole little town getting small below me. Someday, I'd think, I'll get out of here. I won't even remember the name of this place—Whitson, California, all dust and wind, out east of the Sierras and lost in the desert.

Truth is, what I'd been thinking a lot about then was Cat's mom, Jackie. She was young, and she worked nights serving cocktails at the Snug Harbor. She had a voice that rasped a little from too many cigarettes and dark eyes that looked right into me. She laughed at me and called me Cat's crow. That was OK. She noticed.

I spent most of my time at school thinking about stuff like that, stuff I shouldn't be thinking about. One particular Friday I ditched Cat at lunch. I liked her and everything but didn't think I had to escort her around all the time. I walked her home, and she didn't say anything, but I knew she was pissed by the way she kept staring off into space. Cat's the kind that has a little-girl voice, little-girl face, blue eyes, a few freckles on her nose, all that and the tight little body of a woman. Corner of Bry and Fifth, she stopped and looked at some local band's flyer flapping on a telephone pole as if she were trying to memorize it. And then she just ran off.

Watching her fade down the street, yellow hair like a struck match against the buildings and the signs and the little creepy park there, made me feel lonesome. But you know, it felt right. Actually, Cat is, like most girls, a pain in the butt. Besides, it was Friday and time to play. I thought it would work out better that way; I didn't want her along. She was better off left out of the mess the Ravens had planned.

3. My Mom

"Cat. Caaaatheeeriiine! Catherine. Where are my black hose? Sweet pea, you know, the ones with the little red hearts?"

As if I'd ever wear that kind of thing. I said, "Mom. They are wherever you left them!" You see, I had developed a style of my own that I got mostly from BBC reruns on public television. Plaid schoolgirl skirts, clean white blouses. I thought the English very refined.

"Look for them, honey. Mom's late."

At that moment I wasn't too interested in Jackie's nylons *or* her date, as it had occurred to me that Jason had purposely made me mad at lunch, knowing I wouldn't speak to him. Obviously he and the guys, his *Ravens*, wanted to go somewhere by themselves.

Just then the doorbell rang. I rolled from the couch and switched off the tube, an old Jane Fonda flick from the sixties, Jane acting out some Hollywood writer's pot fantasy of Barbie in space. I stopped at the door to pull my hair back, catching myself in the entry mirror, a little surprised at how tired I looked—dark raccoon rings and all. When I cracked open the door, there was a tall black man checking me out with a slow, pleasant grin, his face smooth as a pecan. Bright, perfect teeth.

"Hello," he said, rolling it off his tongue like gospel.

"Hello," I said, opening the door and stepping back. "Mom's almost ready."

"Mom is a sweet name for Jackie," he said, looking at me with big chestnut eyes.

I kept staring at his skin. It was shining. Not with sweat or anything, it just shone, and I wanted to touch it, the way, at times, I'll want to touch a baby's head but don't. Usually I didn't pay any attention to my mother's dates. For as long as I could remember they had been parading in and out of our front door.

Some nights I would fall asleep on the couch. Sleeping there, I would often stir and dream—I started sleeping on the couch when I was seven, drifting off to the white fuzz of the telly, the Brits say "telly"—listening to their voices clinking like the ice cubes in their drinks from the other side of the kitchen door, the sounds sifting into my sleep. I would think of my mother as royalty in exile, and because of her responsibility to her refugee subjects, she had to entertain nightly whether she liked to or not.

Even now I think of my mother as a queen of some kind. I can see why they came around. I suspected she'd even caught Jason's eye. She had a way of making you feel like you were the only one in the world because when you spoke, her eyes never left yours. And she smiled and tilted her head back and laughed softly even when there was no joke, and it teased you out of taking yourself so seriously. It made you feel light. It must've made all those lonely men feel like kings for a while. That's why I can't hate her for it. For her, it was a kind of calling. Though, sometimes, I wonder why she needed *that* much attention.

4. The Boost

Raven—a large, intelligent black bird of prey with shiny, lustrous feathers characterized by a raucous caw; muscular, mischievous, chiefly carnivorous.

Six o'clock and I was skimming down Fifth, the wind cool, coming off the street with that sweet diesel smell, sky white with runny red ink spilled across it. I was lord of the streets and all that silence except for my wheels humming beneath me, the buildings flashing alongside. Bernard had me cornered for half an hour that night, going on about the importance of Education, so I was late. When I rounded the corner at Market, I could see the steeple of St. Peter's stabbing the yellow clouds there, and I cranked hard banking my turn, my left arm dragging, the knuckles of my gloved hand grazing the pavement. I pulled up and spun backward, bending one knee, braking pointedly with my right blade, and bowed to the boys. They whistled low in appreciation. I liked that because to me skating is everything. Bladers all, they knew what kind of time it takes to learn it.

"Where's Cat?" they wanted to know.

"I dunno. Doesn't matter. Miscreants, let's jam."

We skated, with the quick, choppy jerks of puppets, skirted the side of the cathedral, and dropped to the ground at the rear of the place in between a couple of blue Dumpsters tagged, recently I'd noticed, with RIGHTEOUS CHAOS in a purple phosphorescent scrawl. Since it was Doug that first spotted the place, I let him call the shots. He squinted at the roof, its shadow towering over us, and measured his words.

"Karendeep, you stay here. If anything happens or anybody comes, you skate out front and give us a whistle as loud as you can. Start up and don't stop till we're all clear of here." Karendeep, who wore a black turban that pulled his wide black eyebrows back in a startled stare, and who usually said no more than three words in a row, nodded once. "Ozzie, you circle the front and the sides and keep a sharp eye."

Ozzie was a weird kid with stiff albino hair that kinked from the top of his head in spirals. He had moldy green dimes for eyes that were always searching to the sides of his head and skin that burned, too easily, to a strange brick red. His nails were nearly always nipped short to bleeding. We called him crack-baby, though if the flat truth were said, he was just nervous and, like us, an honorable, straight D student. If you ask me, his mom and dad were totally normal folks who doted on him constantly so he had no excuse for himself, except maybe having been born on the same block as the rest of us and needing something to do to make him feel part of something bigger than himself.

Doug looked at me. I was staring back at him hard, so he nodded in a salute of respect when he said, "You and I, we'll do it."

Doug and I had known each other so long I didn't

10

remember not knowing him. He was a skinny, awful-looking kid when he was little, with horse-sized choppers and tiny black eyes. He was always picking at the little heat zits he'd get on his fat strawberry nose in the summer, and I generally had to beat him up at least once a week to keep him from telling me what to do. He was a know-it-all. Didn't matter what you wanted to talk about, he'd run off at the mouth about how you had it almost right except for the fact that . . . And then he'd surprised everyone by growing up into that big face of his and looking like a movie star—athletic, dark, a killer smile that he used all the time to get his way. He'd just started to feel the power he had with girls and had been practicing this funny way of dropping his head so that some of his hair half hid his eyes, and then he'd look out at you through the hair with all this phony charm. He didn't know that if he looked at me like that again, I was going to have to pop him.

"OK," I said, "let's do it." And then, I don't know why, I heard this thrash sound of skater punk going off with a vengeance in my head as we slipped, quick as mice, around the side of the building, pushed the door open, and iced across the marble tiles, up the aisle to the altar where the mikes were—all quality stuff.

We snatched them, careful to roll up the cords and the jacks. There was a faint, burnt smell of incense, and the blue and green light from the windows made Doug's face look like it was underwater. I felt really alive. Doug pump-skated to the rear of that barn and started clunking up the stairs to the choir loft. I knew he was after a little booster amp up there that was fed by an old organ. He was clunking and pulling himself up by the banister rail, and I thought we must be freakin' out of our heads when Ozzie, I guess it was Ozzie, started whistling and then shouting our names like some kind of nitwit.

So I zipped like a bullet over to one of the windows and cracked the old iron latch and poked my nose out to see a cop car roll up and squeak hard to a stop, some kind of sci-fi star-spangled cockroach, chrome antennas bristling in the streetlamps, red eyes spinning furiously. This was *not* TV. That was Doug clattering around in the loft like a trapped animal and me feeling like my head was pumped full of bad, ear-bleeding guitar.

5. Abigail

In the dead pull of this watery dream, I'm swirling, facedown, arms outstretched; Abigail, my sister, is my mirror, her body sinking beneath me. Her fingertips graze mine, though she's lost in her dream of oblivion, her eyes, already those of the blind, fleshy and white. Bubbles rise in silent Os from her lips, which are as pale as the shells of abalone, her figure, a kite that flutters, wavering, a bird hesitating, then pulled into wind. She folds into herself, collapsing, as if changing elements the way paper burns clean to air and is gone. I am still mortal and helpless, a line from the Psalms stitching a thread through my heart: "Thou hast made me as handbreadths / And my lifetime as nothing in thy sight," *and I feel the hands of the father I've never known—how do I know it is my father?— take hold and pull me, screaming, into the world.*

6. Baby Saul

I woke the next day with a start like somebody had jabbed me or something, eyes snapping open. I thought about calling Cat but didn't. I just stayed there in bed, working this out, how it must have been that day for him, Baby Saul. His life wasn't so different from mine that I couldn't do it and get it right. I'd been a little guy like him once. Same neighborhood. Same streets. Same shit.

I took my time with it. I thought, probably, he would've got up yesterday like anybody, took a shower, watched the water spinning into the drain. Maybe he whistled. Maybe not. He brushed his teeth carefully—no, probably did it too fast, doing the usual lousy job kids do if nobody's watching them. I suppose his mom laid out a bowl of cereal, or maybe she was already gone to work and he did it himself. There really isn't anything spectacular about being eight years old in a little town, two hundred miles straight in from the coast, out in the boonies, in a place that rotted before it came to anything—where Baby Saul and I were supposed to be growing up. I wonder if he hated this town like I do.

He walked the sixteen blocks to Lane Elementary, probably watching the blackbirds jumping on the lawns. Played kickball at recess, scored pretty well, and felt fine for the rest of the afternoon. I know Ishmael, his brother, would've picked him up, because Ishmael already had

14

wheels. No license, but a very fine old Impala, clean and stock because his grandfather kept it that way until he gave it to him. Ishmael and I used to be friends, up until the seventh grade, when he faded out of my circle. He had become one of the true hard cases our school could claim. Rumor was he stole cars and I don't know what all, but he had a crew that followed him, and no one dared mess with them. They weren't big-time criminals, but they were serious enough.

I imagined that Baby Saul stuck one of those finger-mess paintings he made that day to the refrigerator and slammed out the screen door to horse around until dark. But it was last night standing in an alley that I pictured him, standing looking up at a patch of sky between the buildings behind the cathedral where the clouds were bunched in like greasy rags. He had a white T-shirt on with his skinny arms showing and cutoffs that dropped below his knees. And he was just staring, the way kids do when they're not thinking anything, just taking in their life however it comes.

That's how it was when I rounded the corner. I was alone, 'cause when the cops came, we panicked and split off in every direction. I was almost flying, almost clear of what I never wanted and what was about to get me. I hit him. Hard. His legs spun away from him, and he tumbled away from me, slamming to the pavement. I reeled around, quick as death itself, and saw him lying there, blood running from his ear as if it had never had any loyalty to him at all and was happy to be free of his head. I knew he was dead. I didn't want to know that. But it was pretty clear. And then, right there, something happened, just the kind of thing you can't predict or judge or say anything about until you yourself are there. You know, I went cold through my whole body. And my mind, it was as clear as water then, not confused at all, and I thought only of myself and what I must do to save my skin. And that hasn't changed.

7. Hate

Something happened. When I staggered off the couch and swung into the kitchen, there was Barry munching Wheaties. He managed the best smile he could under the circumstances, what with his mouth puffed full and the little pearls of milk bright on his fine black chin. He rolled his eyes and winked theatrically. I spun a fast getaway U-turn and was out of there. I was in a long—oh, God—*purple* T-shirt with BUGS BUNNY plastered all over it. It just covered my panties.

I dashed upstairs, feeling the blood draining away from my face, which surely he'd seen flushing red as Jackie's worst nail polish, Night of Passion. I nearly ran through the shower, then slowed to primp a little in the mirror. Changed tops three times, settling on a simple muslin in a soft orange orchid. I spritzed a little of Jackie's perfume on my neck, changed my mind, and tried rubbing it off with a towel. I tiptoed past Jackie's room, listening for signs of consciousness, though that was unlikely. Saturdays she usually slept in.

When I reentered the kitchen, royalty ready for tea, I graced him with a cool "Good morning."

"Good morning," he said. "Didn't mean to fluster you any."

I sighted him down my nose with a whatever-could-you-mean?

"Scare you—I didn't mean to scare you."

My confidence fading, I turned to the fridge, fumbling for milk.

"Jackie won't be up for hours," I said coolly. The milk was gone. I turned, trying to eye him accusingly, though it didn't seem to have any effect.

He smiled broadly, confident, innocent, genuine. "Come on, I'll run you to the store." He stood to put his dish in the sink and ran the water after it. He turned his head to see me. "You look nice," he said in his easy, open way. He *knew* I'd go. Who was this guy?

He had this beautiful old sun-colored Buick. It had to be fifteen years old, at least, though flawless. He told me he was good with tools and engines and stuff, and his car did hum like it was alive and liked to be running. He saw that I liked that, said he was impressed I could appreciate such a thing and maybe sometime he would let me take it out with him and teach me to drive if Jackie gave the OK. That was pretty optimistic of him. I'd give him three weeks with Jackie. Max. He obviously wasn't dumb. Perhaps he was what he seemed, a nice guy or smitten. That I understood, since I was the same way about Jason— where the heck *was* Jason last night, anyway?

We were passing the mall when out of the blue I asked if we could stop. I knew it was selfish, but I knew, too, that he was willing to make a good impression, and I needed a new skirt and I wanted to wear it Monday. We stopped.

We were walking around Sears looking at all the stuff I couldn't really afford. But I tried on all the ladies' Lon-

18

don Fog raincoats, and Barry said I looked smashing with my blond hair fluffed out over the collar. "Smashing, daaarling," he kidded. Frankly, I loved the attention.

Nothing really grabbed me—all the skirts were too short or too long, too Whitson—except this red woolen beret I thought might look good floating by when I skated. Barry bought it for me. He insisted. I was hesitating about the whole thing, but the saleslady kept hovering around and looking at me and looking at Barry. I thought she thought we couldn't afford anything, so I said, in my best British, "Yes, dear, this will do. Don't you think?" letting my voice climb the end of a sentence in the lilting, plaintive way the English do.

Well, at that she started blinking and then frowned and rang us up a bit too quickly, I thought. Anyway, we were walking to the car, and I was sashaying around, pulling the cap down at different angles, prancing a few feet in front of Barry and striking these crazy *Vogue* poses for him. When I think of it now, I guess I was acting like Jackie. I felt very fine because Barry was laughing and saying things such as "Go, girl," and "Uh-huh!"

Barry was very good-looking, and I was surprised to find myself enjoying the way his laugh and his smile felt warm all around me like the sun coming out first thing in the morning. All of a sudden I heard these brakes screeching, and then this thud, and as if in slow motion, I saw Barry push away from the hood of this truck that had just come to a halt there. It was one of those ugly pickups with oversized tires, stuff patched all over the fenders. Two skinny guys in white T-shirts were in it. From the window the driver stuck his head out, yellow straw sprouting from his chin in a failed attempt at a beard, I guess, his head shaved very close and shiny.

"Oh, excuse me." He grinned. Strawface spit a wad of chewing tobacco to the ground, saying, "You better git on home, girlie." The guy riding shotgun started choking on his snot and his laughter. They were seriously gross.

Barry crossed to me quickly. "C'mon. Let's go."

His fingers were digging into my arm as we hurried over the two parking lanes to our car and hopped in. Barry hit the starter, and the engine rolled on with a deep-throated willingness, and we pulled out and away. Fortunately, they weren't following.

Nobody was talking, and the car started filling up with a heaviness like air before rain. I was watching Barry carefully out of the corner of my eye, and I could tell he was working something out in his mind because he was chewing his lip and huffing air gently through his nose. I just kept watching the blocks go by, almost invisible because I'd seen them so often.

Suddenly Barry said very quickly as if he wanted to make a point and then be quit of it, "I'm a musician, sweetheart. Got musician's hands. They're my bread and butter. I can't be breaking them up on some fool kid's head." He blew air through his pursed lips. Then he brightened, and the lines on his forehead relaxed into that sleek, touchable wood again.

"You like the blues, kid? I used to play them." He wasn't waiting for an answer. "Not no more. Tenor sax and vocals, and strictly jazz. Once I started playing it, I never looked back. You know, it's like this . . . this cold, heavy river you step into and you feel the water sliding up to your heart and you ease yourself out and let it take you. And then nothing can touch you because *you* ain't you anymore; you're the river and you're part of some power."

He looked over at me, through me really, and his voice had something in it that made me listen when he spoke. "You could look at that river, and it looks the same all day long, but it ain't. It changes; its smooth snake back is moving all the time, building a little here, coiling up tight a little there, then relaxing and flowing on, making its own way toward something and somewhere new, somewhere different. It's there only a second, and then it's gone."

He tapped the steering wheel nervously. "Playing jazz is like that—following that thing that's bigger than yourself." His eyes were on the rearview mirror when he laughed deeply to himself. "You believe that, don't you, kid?"

"I guess so." Actually, I didn't know what to say.

He shook his head. "I'm not sure I do."

I took a chance and said, "Who the heck listens to jazz in this town, anyway?" Our eyes met honestly for the first time, and he laughed, again with a richness that I could tell pleased him, so I laughed, too.

Right then was when I decided I liked Barry. Liked him a lot.

8. The Neighborhood

When we first moved to the neighborhood, I was only nine years old. It was a step back for Bernard, my dad. He lost his job as a trucking dispatcher in South San Francisco, and so we hauled out here one summer to take over Grandmother's old place where he'd grown up. There were only the three of us, but that didn't help because Bernard was a pathological pack rat. I suppose it was losing that job he thought was his for life that did it.

Mom and I just began to notice that nothing would ever be thrown away. If a TV blew, he'd haul it into a corner of a bedroom, saying he could use it for backup parts for the next one. If a dish cracked, he'd save the pieces in a box—good for potting plants to keep the soil loose, though my mother never kept potted plants, just a couple of dried-up oleanders stuck in two barrels on the front porch.

Every nook and cranny of the place was crammed with every kind of worthless junk you can imagine: crooked lamps; electric eggbeaters that no one ever used, even when they still worked; magazines and newspapers stacked in towers; boxes of doorknobs and latches and bits of plumbing. To get around, we had to squeeze through these heaps of stuff in narrow corridors like rats threading their way from food to water to a place to curl up.

22

After years scrounging work as a carpenter, Bernard finally got on at the post office, though that security never seemed to ease his need to hoard what was mostly useless. He still got excited when he hauled home, say, a busted radio from the thirties that he might nab at a yard sale, the kind of thing that is impossible to fix because there aren't any more tubes anywhere to make it run. Didn't matter. He'd cram it in the corner of the bathroom, where he could drip shaving cream and water on it every morning and marvel at his cunning and good fortune.

Our house is still downtown to the west of the main streets. Since the time my dad was a kid, warehouses and shops sprang up behind the few residential blocks that once made up the original town. The buildings are old—brick, a few wooden Victorians that didn't burn in any of the fires this city has had, looking like dry wedding cakes, and some small wood and stucco bungalows with short lawns that run only a few feet to the street.

My mom worked at Walgreen's and spent most of her free time writing letters to her five sisters. Nothing ever happened, so you got me as to what she was writing about. Never mind, though, she was at it every evening. Either that or she'd be embroidering doilies for the West Front Street Care Center, an old folks' home that I would guess had maybe five thousand white doilies draped all over God knows where.

Bernard had a groove carved through the crap piled in the garage to a stool and a small piece of workbench he cleared there, just enough room for a bottle and one shot glass kept hidden in a red toolbox that Mom and I gave him for Christmas one year. When I think of Bernard, it's of him sitting there in the light from a bare bulb overhead, and he's staring into his pile of junk, feeling some kind of mysterious comfort coming from all that dead metal and paper and wood.

It'd been just over a week since that bad night when me and the Ravens ditched the cops. We didn't meet up then till hours later at the dugout behind the baseball field. I mean, no one saw what happened there in the alley, and I didn't blab, but I didn't feel safe anymore. I needed to get the whole thing out of my mind—that kid's head cracked on concrete—so I tried to push it down deep, let my mind blank out. Trouble was, I thought Doug might know. He'd seen how tweaked I was later when we were looking over the little bit of gear we'd managed to cart off.

There's only one thing about a secret, and that's if even one other person knows it, it ain't a secret. So I was waking up at night, going out back to watch the stars up there, cold and quiet and telling me exactly nothing as usual. All week I'd worked on Cat, laying out a plan to live with Jackie and her for a while. At first she didn't see the point, and I wasn't going to explain why I was so jumpy. She did understand how I couldn't stomach my folks, and she eventually got behind the idea. Said she'd have to work on Jackie and to give her some time.

In the evenings, jeez, in that house, with Bernard and his booze and Mom with her worry, their faces, hanging all over the place like torn paintings, gave me some kind of dread I just couldn't take anymore. So I left. And you know, when I did, other than make them a little nervous about what might happen when the school or some other authority called, things went on just as they always did, at least for them, I suppose. They traded away their lives for a little peace. I left them to it.

9. The Arrangement

That Jason came to live with us then was not a coincidence. It's the kind of thing that happens for a reason. I mean, who could have predicted that his folks would let him? It wasn't a surprise that Jackie said OK. She'd left home at sixteen herself, so Jason staying with us for a while didn't faze her at all.

His folks dropped by after the first week he was there to talk to Jackie and nose around. Mostly they just sat on the couch and looked distressed while Jackie walked about the room, throwing herself in poses she thought elegant, all the while chattering in fits and starts like Marilyn Monroe on barbiturates.

They thought Jason was in a phase. That it'd be best if he stayed with us if he wanted. They thought he'd become *irrational*—that was their word—if they forced him to live at home. They might have been right. They thought him exceptionally bright, even a genius, maybe, and therefore extraordinarily sensitive and best left to his own lead. I don't know about being a genius. Jason *was* very smart, though a complete mess at school, and he mostly spoke to me in monosyllables. I was always at the top of my class—straight *A*s without trying. I thought maybe Jason would improve his schoolwork living with us. Though I didn't know about that, either. I think, now, he liked making *D*s and hanging out with his misfit friends.

26

Jackie made a big deal of the fact that Jason sleep in his own room and that there be no hanky-panky. That was definitely a bit of theater on Jackie's part. She couldn't pass up the opportunity to play conventional mom. She knew perfectly well I had no intention of doing anything like *that* until I was in my thirties, at least. I had no notion of serving drinks to dullards in some dim-lit lounge for the rest of my life. Finally, they left, his mother blinking back tears, promising to phone every weekend.

Barry was coming around a lot, decked out in his panther-black good looks and padding around the house, a smooth show biz type. He had a jazz combo, the Slow Elephant, that had been playing the Snug Harbor for a couple of months, so he worked evenings and now was going to hang out at our house on weekends, I guessed. He even stopped by on a Wednesday to make breakfast for me and Jackie. He made these huge omelets with mushrooms, whistling bebop faster than I've ever heard a human being whistle.

I've got to say I admired his style. He was always dressed in these smashing, to-die-for outfits—silk maroon shirts, natty trousers. He was the kind of man women notice. The kind that will make your voice catch just by smiling at you. I was unsure now if I would be unhappy or not when Jackie let him go.

You know, the thing about coincidences is that though things happen for a reason, it's almost never the one you're thinking at the time.

10. Settling In

The first thing you noticed about Cat's house, Jackie's house, I mean, were the cats. They had a gray cat that moved around like smoke, that quiet, and three white and liver-spotted ones from the same litter. They crashed around the place all the time, real sultans of leisure.

I think cats are cool because they've got two worlds—house and outdoors. A cat will rip the head off a sparrow it's been torturing for the last half hour and then come indoors and curl up on your lap as if it were your baby. I think they're closer to the earth like women and their moon thing every month and their fussing in the garden and with their food and their preening. I always knew when my Cat was about to start in on my Inability to Communicate because she started easing around the room, touching the furniture until she was sliding up alongside me just like a cat flicking its tail.

I liked how the whole house smelled of lilacs and soap. That was Jackie. Jackie's another story. All I'll say is that she was sexy and funny, with thick dark hair. Their place was an old bungalow with a couple of rooms and a second bathroom tacked on top and a screened porch out back that at one time somebody fitted out with plywood, making a kind of room where I camped. It gets cold at night, even in the desert, but I was hoping I could cut it until summer. I had a down sleeping bag and a TV the

28

size of a toaster, a stack of *National Geographic*s, some comics, and some skater mags, so I'd nothing to complain about. At night I'd just lay there, nodding off, enjoying the cats crying outside, noticing how it seemed like they made the sounds of human babies.

11. Night

Once Jason moved in, I abandoned the couch and started sleeping upstairs in my room. Often I would lie awake in bed and consider the risks of sleeping, as I did, with my head to the wall, the east wall. I wondered if it was bad for your brain if you slept arranged in that way, head going down and feet rising as they must, imperceptibly, as the earth turns ever so slowly toward morning. I had long considered moving my bed sideways, I mean north to south, so that I would spin that way, side to side instead of end over end. Maybe when I went to university in London, I'd be the first to research the effects of all the different ways of arranging yourself when you slept.

You know the problem with growing up is that you discover things about the world, about yourself, that aren't always pleasant. I bet Jackie or Barry knew things about themselves they couldn't admit anymore, even to themselves. I imagined a person could get to the point where nothing could happen that would get through to them the way it really was. I thought, too often people arrange things in their heads to suit themselves. And then I started wondering if everything was just happening in your head and not outside you. And if that was true, I wondered if what I was thinking—I mean, just then I was imagining Barry driving around in his car in the middle of the night, whistling himself into his river—I wondered if that was really happening because I was thinking it, and I saw it was, in a way, like that, and it scared me.

Sometimes I wondered if my sister was alive only when I remembered her. I thought that maybe that was the truth, and I knew I had to make a habit of seeing her, vividly, so she could get out and around once in a while and take what little pleasure I could give her. Sometimes I just lay in my bed imagining the whole world into being, all the people and the animals and the houses and the fat moon, and I let the earth spin me any way it wanted because the world had a lot of dangers, and I couldn't be bothered with every little thing all the time.

# 12. School

"How much?" I shouted at Doug over the earsplitting buzz of the late bell. We were standing in the dark of the halls of Emerson High.

"You heard me, Jason. Eighty bucks," he said, spitting it out, shifting from one foot to the other, a cocky underweight boxer. "You know we had to leave the amp when we ditched the cops. It was only the mikes and jacks I could sell."

It had been just over two weeks since we snatched the stuff, and Doug had finally unloaded it. Ozzie came tripping over to us, head half cocked down like a dog on to a scent. He snapped to attention and gave me a corny salute.

"Well, I don't want any of it," I said.

"How come?" he said, squinting and searching my face for a clue he expected to find.

"Want any of what?" Ozzie questioned, clueless as usual.

"Just don't."

"OK. But I thought we could buy some gear for the Ravens or some black concert T-shirts that matched or something."

"Whatever." I shrugged. "Do what you want." Mr. Davies was standing in the doorway to English One, curling his forefinger at me and scrunching one eye and loading the other up with all the evil get-your-sorry-butt-in-here he could manage. I started toward him, Ozzie dogging my heels, so I stopped quickly to let him bump into me. "Ozzie, what are you doing? Aren't you late for math or something?" I said.

"Oh, yeah, right." He saluted and beat it down the hall as if being on time somewhere was a terrific new idea.

I followed Davies into class and took my seat as some of the girls in the class stared at me with their pitiful, snot-nosed scowls.

Parker Thurston Davies was this huge beat-up guy in his late fifties that suffered from the delusion that he could scare people into learning. His face, stretched back at the corners, looked like he had massive acne when he was a kid or else maybe he got burned and they botched the skin grafts. He was the sort of guy that could be very friendly to you at times, and just when you'd relaxed around him, he'd say something smart-mouthed and embarrass you in front of everyone. He was like an oversized wrestler. That was because when he paced before the class, rolling his shoulders and stabbing the air, weaving a little, he looked as if he might dive down and head-butt you in the knees.

A lot of the time he liked to try to shock us, telling about the time he lay on a pile of dead soldiers in Vietnam for three entire days until somebody figured out he hadn't croaked and medevaced him out to civilization and cute nurses etc. Actually, part of his head *was* made of metal, a fact he liked to remind us of occasionally by drawing himself up to his full six-four and plinking his forehead with his thumb, saying, "I will not be mocked." Plink, plink. "Now, get to work!"

I would have completely written him off except that Cat felt sorry for him and always defended him. Of course, she would. He treated her like a princess once he discovered she had actually read Dylan Thomas—some dead poet. The guy was totally nuts over him. I think if the school board would've let him, he would have had a little altar in the corner of the room with a picture and votive candles and everything. I dunno, I thought maybe Dylan Thomas would mean something to me when I was MATURE or something, but I wouldn't advise anyone to hold their breath.

Davies gave us a good dose once in a while, but mostly when all that rhyme and meter got going, I started feeling seasick and just put my head down on the desk and thought about skating. About Baby Saul. What Ishmael might do to me. The future. It's a bad feeling when all you want to do is go back and not forward, and your head feels like one huge bruise with a loop inside it that keeps playing back to you a picture of a little kid sprawled on the pavement, and that kid's got blood snaking from his head, dark as dreadlocks.

13. Skating

It is a verifiable fact, statistically speaking, that there are very few English who skate. I never was attracted to it because as a rule I'm not very athletic. To tell you the cross-my-heart truth, it was the one thing I could get Jason to talk about. Back then Jason was thin, almost lanky. I liked to watch the chiseled lines of his chin that hung, narrow and wolflike, when he spoke. And how his eyes lit up into a washed wrung-out blue that burned cool like little gas jets when he talked about skating and was happy for a moment. You could tell he really wanted you to understand when he explained how it made him feel, how difficult it was to get smooth and able at it. Personally, I thought everyone should have a passion. Mine, of course, was the English.

I'd seen Jane Austen's *Emma* and *Pride and Prejudice* on television, and they sparked my interest. After that I read anything English I could get my hands on in the Whitson public library. And I was a full-fledged devotee of the BBC series *Mystery*.

Someday I was going to London, and I vowed I would walk beside the Thames, that ancient river running right through the city to the sea. I would be wearing this gorgeous long overcoat and writing letters home full of all the fabulous stuff I heard the Brits saying to one another. I even taped a map of the country to the wall near my bed, and I could imagine all the people there moving around with their pink faces in the fog and drizzle. Anyway, what a switch for me to spend my saved money on skate gear. That just goes to show you that you never know what's going to happen next in your life.

At first it killed me. The muscles in my thighs and my calves would start twitching at night like long rubber bands pulled tight and then let loose to thrum. The first day we ever skated together way back in September right after we first met, long before he moved in with Jackie and me, Jason had shown me the park, *his* park, he'd said. It was on Miramar, where there are these acres of cement walkways and concrete planters that twist through shrubs and flowers. And there, patiently, he had taught me to skate. It wasn't the skating but his devotion to it, his capacity for seriousness, that made me fall for him. Even now I can admire that.

Often we went there in the evenings because there weren't many people then and we could do what we wanted without somebody calling the police and spoiling everything. I thought it funny how adults wanted us to do something besides watch the telly, but then couldn't seem to wait to ruin things once we did find something to do. They didn't know that being a skater was having something all yours, something that wouldn't fail you when you're feeling ugly and down. I learned that from Jason. Every skate was a journey with small surprises and challenges to test yourself, to see what you were made of.

Jason had practiced obsessively and was a pro by local standards, but he was very patient with me. Once, at the very end of that January, we went to the park by ourselves without the Ravens. We were skating very slowly, tracing huge looping sixes and eights. The trees were thin black silhouettes, and the air had a crispness in it that was a kind of happiness edged with sadness all around it. Maybe because he was living with us, I could feel him, understand what he was then—this mix of hurt and anger, smoothed over by the rhythm of our skating, smoothed the way water is as it passes slowly over rocks. You know the rocks down there are hard and sharp, but they're hidden, and so the water ripples gently, and it calms you.

I slid up to him, close, leaning into him, and we skated together, matching step for step, and I wished we could go on that way forever, though, like most happiness I've known, it lasted only a moment.

14. The Fight

You know, sometimes when the wind has been scrambling across desert, high desert, with nothing to stop it but sagebrush and a few scraggy cottonwoods, the sky goes a smeared brown. And after a few days dust settles over everything. It drops on the porches and the sidewalks so when people walk around, they leave, like animals do, little traces of their coming and going. It settles on the car tops, on the plateglass windows downtown, on the mailboxes at the corners, on the dry leaves of the shrubs, and even on every dried-up blade of grass of all of the tired little lawns that make up this sorry town.

Folks in Whitson put on a fake indifference to what Cat says is a reminder of the biblical power of the desert (she actually *read* the Bible). I don't know about that, but the whole town does go quiet for a few days until the wind stops, and then pretty soon people come out, a few at a time, nodding to one another with their faces bunched up and wiping away tears from the grit they can't seem to get from their eyes.

At the end of a day like that the Ravens were finally out together again—mostly because folks were at home and the streets were ours. The fine sand in the streets made our blades less reliable, and it was hard going at times, picking up any speed.

It was the first day that Jackie pulled the tiny surgical steel post from my ear and pushed through a tiny lightning bolt of gold I'd bought from the majorly obese lady downtown at the local head shop, where she sold all kinds of nearly illegal stuff. Jackie had first done the piercing on the weekend before, with all the Ravens gathered around in the kitchen to watch.

We were heading over to one of our favorite weekend spots, a half street that dead-ended behind a club on Seventh. The few local bands played there on weekends, and we liked sitting out back and listening and watching the small crowd, mostly working guys, house painters, plumbers, cement layers—that kind—and their women milling about outside. There were some older buildings and a cement loading dock across the alley that had stairways and iron handrails that we liked to skate off and grind down, doing tricks and generally messing around.

We were skating as fast as conditions would allow when we came around the corner, heading toward the lone streetlamp that marked our resting spot with a cone of yellow. Ozzie, Cat, Doug, and Karendeep were all fanned out behind me like wingmen to my lead. As we approached the stop there, we jumped, jamming our knees to our chests and landing at the top of the stairs. Doug was last up, and his blades grazed the top step, rolling him in a heap. He rose weakly, then collapsed, cussing and swinging his arms and looking around at us. Nobody said anything. I reached down to help him up, but he pushed me away.

Karendeep stepped in. "Here, I'll get him." His eyes met mine. I stepped away, and he leaned over to haul Doug up and Doug let him. Whatever, I thought.

For months we'd been using candles to wax the

handrails coming off the dock, since they were the best grind rails in town and we liked to keep them ready and slick. "Doug," I said, "I've got a little treat for you."

"Ooh, a little treat for you," cooed Ozzie, winking at everybody. Goofy.

"Ooh," they all chimed in, trying to goad me, being stupid.

I skated to the end of the dock, spun around, and came back full speed. I leaped, raising one leg, grabbing the toe of my skate with my right hand, and landing my back skate on the top of the rail, greasing the pipe with ease and grace. I touched down at the bottom of the stairs, cut a half circle, and laughed, looking Doug in the face. What I'd done was a fishbrain, don't ask me why they call it that, but it was difficult enough to impress most anybody.

Doug took the bait and dusted his hands on his pants and rolled his shoulder like a major-league hitter warming up. Cat said, "Doug, you don't have to prove anything."

"Oooh, Doug, you don't got nothin' to proooove," Ozzie chortled. We all laughed, even Cat and Doug. "C'mon, Doug, do a fahrvergnugen!" Ozzie shouted, his little eyes shining.

"Do it," said Karendeep evenly.

"Yeah, I'd like to see that." And I meant it, and if Doug had it in him, well then, good.

Doug took off, turned slowly at the end of the dock, and started back, coming on, gathering speed. He lifted quickly into the air, pivoting sideways neatly, both skates perpendicular to the rail, leaning his ankle and his body into the downslope for a perfect, big-time grind. He tore off the rail with considerable force, twisted face forward again, and landed, jouncing, rolling hard. Cat and Karendeep jumped up and started clapping. Ozzie bounced in circles, chanting, "Oh, man! Oh, man!" like the Cat in the Hat on acid or something. Doug was beaming his best prep school grin, all teeth, his black hair falling forward over his face.

"I been practicing," he said, searching my face.

I liked that he wanted my approval. I was impressed. But I was *always* practicing. Doug never even had a thought about skating that I hadn't had a hundred times before.

"Watch," I instructed. Then to Cat and the rest: "Watch."

This time I rose into the air, my whole body angled forward thirty degrees or so, the grind plate of my right skate catching the rail at that angle. Quick, I crossed my left leg over the right and grabbed the toe of my boot with my right hand. It's more than hard to grind leaning downhill, but with your legs crossed, ankles bent, one foot in the air, it's . . . well, try it sometime. I shot free of the rail, twirled in the air, unfurling my legs, touching down like an ice skater—a genuine, professionally executed rocket torque.

Everybody was quiet, Karendeep shaking his head in disbelief. Doug's eyes were slits, and his lips pushed out like garden slugs, fat with wet weather. Cat smiled, her pretty eyelashes beating. Ozzie came forward to high-five me. I tweaked his ear, and he backed off. "Let's kick it," I said, coolly, the king again and for the moment satisfied with myself.

I sat down. Everybody did likewise. Ozzie pulled out some smokes and lit up. We watched this new habit without saying anything, pretending not to notice. He got the damn thing lit and started pulling on it heavily. His eyes were tearing, and he released a thick cloud with something close to agony. He was squinching his eyes to keep out the smoke, so he looked either sleepy or stupid. He took a few more drags and then tossed it into the street, where we watched it brighten for a second in the wind and then die. "Stale. Gotta get some fresh ones." He coughed out the words.

Cat was sitting close to me, and I was enjoying the warmth of her, and I was thinking of biting the back of her neck. The sounds of the band in the club started thumping off the buildings, and I shouted to the Ravens, "Who's up for some real excitement?" They all stared at me blankly. "Anybody?" I demanded.

Doug seemed to be nursing some envy when he looked at me, his eyes narrow.

"Who said you always call the shots, anyway?" He looked surprised that he had said it. I just looked away.

He went on. "How come you're always telling us what to do?"

I held my breath, waiting for somebody to remind him that I didn't always tell everybody what to do, but nobody was talking.

"Hey, guys, we're all friends here," Karendeep said as if to everyone, but he was looking at me.

42

"Give it a rest, Doug," I offered.

"Why should I? You think you're the only person that ever owned a pair of blades?" He paused, chewing his lip, then: "How come, if you're so hot, you go around smashing into people all the time? You know, somebody could get *killed*."

I didn't even blink. There wasn't any reason then to lay off him or to talk him down. I just wanted him to shut his trap, so I pulled myself up and spun around and kicked him square in the belly, my blades sticking him hard. He curled over, and I skated to him quickly and fell on him, smashing his gut with my knees. I let fly two or three solid punches with my fist to his face, grabbed his head, and shook it hard. That was it. He just lay there, his chest heaving, not seriously hurt but finished.

Cat looked at me with my mother's face. Karendeep was kneeling by Doug, muttering, "Jeez, Jason." Ozzie was pale and looked away. Everyone quiet, except Doug breathing like he might vomit.

Out of nowhere Ozzie said, slowly, "Hey. Hey . . . Cat, isn't that . . . Barry?"

Our eyes flicked across the alley toward the back of the club. There in the blue light falling from a bulb over the back door was Barry, and he had a long black woman, shimmering in a green dress, in his arms, and they were kissing.

15. Trouble

Come Monday night I felt I had to talk to Jason about what he'd done to Doug, but he was pecking my closed eyelids softly and I was having difficulty thinking. I was feeling warm and dreamy. In the background the telly murmuring. How was I to know that Jackie had come from work early and was just then opening the back door and putting some groceries down? Suddenly I felt Jason's tongue begin to explore the roof of my mouth, and it gave me a strange tickling sensation. I wanted to laugh. I pulled away. He sighed and pushed his head into my neck like a puppy, kissing my throat. I let my head settle back in some kind of innocent animal pleasure. I looked down at his head, noting the way his new earring sparked in the light. Little thistle of fire, I thought.

"Well, well, well, what have we here?" came Jackie's voice, piercing, cold. Jason sat bold upright, and I looked as casually as I could at Jackie. "Well?" she repeated.

Neither of us said anything. Jason wiped his hair back and stared at the rings on the coffee table. I watched Jackie, trying to decide what scene she was about to play. She crossed the room and sat down quietly in the big easy chair there and pulled her long black hair back across the top of her head, letting it fall slowly over her forehead, where it picked up the light. Jackie loved her hair. She tossed it back, staring pointedly at me when she said,

"Jason, suppose you take a walk and cool off? Give us girls a chance to have a little chat." Jason was struck dumb, I guess, because he rose obediently and left out the back through his room.

"Mom, leave it alone."

"Now, as much as I'd like that," she said, "you know I can't."

"Oh, yes, you can. There is *nothing* to discuss."

"Are you sure about that, Catherine? Nothing?"

"You're the one who screwed up your life, not me," I said calmly. I could see her wince and take a quick breath.

"That's right. That's my point, Cat."

"If you're so all fired worried about sex, why do you tramp around here in your nightie all the time? You think Jason doesn't notice? You think I don't notice?" Jackie's mouth dropped; I could see she wasn't expecting that. I hoped I hadn't gone too far.

"Look, sugar, it isn't me sitting on the couch with him when nobody is home."

"Oh, c'mon, Mom. Jason's my boyfriend. He kisses me sometimes. Would you rather we be out somewhere doing it? Kissing," I added quickly. Her eyes left mine, and she began rummaging around in her purse. She found what she was looking for, put it on the coffee table, and pushed it across to me. It was a little aluminum packet. I knew it contained a condom.

"Oh, r*ee*ally, Mom," I spit. I picked the thing up and threw it across the room, where it lodged in the slats of the window blinds. I know I shouldn't have said it, but looking at that awful thing glinting there accusingly, I lost it. "Jason isn't Barry, you know."

She bristled, and her eyes went from the window to mine. "What is that supposed to mean?"

"Jason isn't sleeping in my bed."

"Listen, Catherine. These friends you have, these boys, are pretty fast company. You've just got to be careful." She shook her head. "You know I've always been honest with you. I know I'm not your average mom." Her eyes were little pools that glinted as she spoke. "Cat, I'm the kind of mother I wish I had had. *You* can grow up and be anything you want, and I'll love you for it. And the reason you can grow up and even consider doing what you want is because you've had a different life." Her eyes were searching mine. "You're free to see things as they are or as you'd like them to be. I've always lived my life the way I see fit, and I don't apologize to anyone." She was talking to herself then, eyes on the rug.

"Well, I seem to see things you have failed to notice," I said pointedly. Her head shot up. I had her attention. She cocked it to one side in question.

"For instance, did you happen to notice that Barry's *black*?"

That my mother could move as quickly as she did was more of a shock than her arriving in front of me in one fluid move to slap me, sharp across the face. I wasn't crying. I wasn't really even surprised. Except by my sudden meanness.

16. The Roost

Karendeep was a quiet type, but you weren't to let that fool you 'cause he was just the sort of guy that was noticing everything. His eyes, large and soft, squishy-looking like black olives, moved slowly as if they were hardly bothering to see anything. But, of course, they did. See. Everything. He was the one that got me to lay off Doug because it might bust up the Ravens if I didn't. He was the one that worked with Ozzie when we first got skates because Ozzie couldn't seem to keep up with the rest of us. And then he scored out the perfect place for the Ravens to meet.

Funny, I'd seen the old place possibly my whole life, but it had never clicked as a roost for us. It was OK meeting in the park and on the streets and everything, but how perfect to have somewhere of our own to kick back in. It must've been a hundred years ago that the place was somebody's home, because nobody builds apartments with huge columns and a porch the size of Georgia, with windows you could drive a minivan through. Somewhere along the line, it was split into four apartments, then let go until the tenants couldn't or wouldn't keep it patched together anymore, I guess. So there on the corner of Oak and Van Ness, at the back of a huge lot, built up a good four feet from the street, it was kind of waiting, unnoticed the way most old folks seem to me to be waiting

47

around to be of use to somebody, anybody. And how could we disappoint such a cool old lady?

It was the day after Jackie blew her top 'cause she caught me and Cat on the couch getting friendly, and she was grounded, so I was surprised when she showed. It was after 8:00 P.M. on a Tuesday when we all converged on the corner and as usual hung around waiting for Ozzie to get his lead behind there. Karendeep was watching Cat watch me. I was making small talk with Doug. I tell you, Doug sticking with the Ravens after I pounded him made me respect him. I knew that *I* couldn't let go of our skating thing very easily, and I liked that he couldn't, either. From then on, though, we always sort of stepped around each other, Doug letting his eyes dart across mine only for a second before he looked away. I assumed he understood that if he suspected anything about Baby Saul, he'd better keep it to himself or risk another beating. Still, he gave me the feeling that if I ever looked away too long, I might just notice somebody had slit my throat or something. Ha!

Ozzie came trolling up, fool that he was, trailing cigarette smoke like a little scarf, eyes beat up and bleary. Doug flung a pebble at him that bounced off his jacket, and Ozzie winced in fake pain, then grinned. "OK, I'm here. Just a small problem with the old lady. She's suffering from the notion that I had some important homework. I spread enough math and geography around my room to convince her I was getting serious," he bragged. "Said the TV was interfering with my life ambition of becoming an astronaut, shut the door to my room, and climbed out the window. I got maybe an hour before she notices anything."

"Is your dad on the road again?" Cat asked, genuinely concerned as usual. She was trying to smooth his hair, but it looked as if she was petting an airedale.

"Yeah, he's hauling uranium out in Arizona."

"Ozzie, you've never said a whole sentence that didn't have a lie in it somewhere," Doug said, looking at him half in admiration and half in disgust.

It was true. It was possible that Ozzie had hood-winked his mom. That was believable 'cause she spent most of her time in a trance in front of the tube, eating all these tasty snacks that Ozzie sometimes snagged for us—cheese crackers, vanilla wafers, and the sort. It was just as possible that Ozzie was late for some other reason or wanted to go home in an hour and so the story. Ozzie wasn't exactly a psychopathic liar. You could tell he just liked the way words zipped from his mouth so much he couldn't stop himself. Mostly we ignored him or listened and laughed.

Karendeep was looking up at the old house that in the dark looked a little less friendly than it did in the daylight. My eyes went with his to the second-story windows, which were tall, arched at the top, and shadowed. I glanced at Karendeep. He smiled, what looked like mischief glinting in his old eyes.

"It's time to check this place out," I said.

17. Doubt

I know that girls are supposed to be complicated and all, but I think that isn't the whole truth. Every guy I've ever known has been complicated. They just don't know it. They've got everything bundled up inside them so tightly I think they're afraid they'll spin out of control if they ever stop to notice themselves as anything but cool and calm. The night that we climbed the rotted back steps of the old Manchester Apartments and Jason and Doug forced the door, I think my life got complicated.

We snuck in and ditched our skates in what might have been a kitchen before a fire left the walls with the look of puffed, blackened marshmallows. We could've skated around on the old hardwood floors, but Jason thought we should be quiet the first time there.

I knew the guys left me out sometimes, and frankly, this night I was both glad to be included and a little sorry I wasn't home reading or washing my hair. We snuck around the bottom floor for a while, easing through the rooms, and Ozzie found an old chair in a den and started to bounce in it until he got stuck with a spring, and Jason told him to shut up and quit acting the fool. The old place had high ceilings with long windows that let in a cold, thin moonlight, painting our faces in primitive slashes. We all seemed to be seized with some kind of hunger because we started to root into the closets and the cupboards and everything. There was nothing there but droppings from rodents and cobwebs strung about like cotton candy, but we seemed intent on finding something. Doug tossed a cup he found through a small window at the bottom of the stairs, and I thought for a moment that Jason would start in with him again, but he just scowled.

Finally we got bored and started up the stairs, Jason in the lead, Karendeep and Doug right behind him, me and Ozzie creeping in tow. At the top of the stairs there was hardly any light.

Doug hissed, "Ozzie, give me a match."

Ozzie fumbled in his pockets, then handed him a lighter with an air of false importance and his usual eagerness to please. Doug lit it, and our shadows jumped to the walls, quivering there.

We could see a door at the end of a short hallway. Jason started toward it with abrupt bravado. It was locked. He and Doug shouldered it until it gave way with a loud splinter. We stuck our heads in and scanned inside, where there was a large bedroom with windows all around, a little bench built into one wall. There was an old iron bed and a smelly mattress that somebody had dragged to one corner.

Jason entered, stooped, and brushed his hand through some cigarette butts and dust there on the floor. "Somebody was here," he said matter-of-factly.

We gathered around as he groped through the ashes. We looked around the room. Moonlight in long swords.

Cobweb chandeliers. Our faces—eerie pumpkins, disembodied.

"So is this somebody's place already?" Ozzie coughed weakly.

"No. These butts are way cold, stupid," Jason snapped dryly. "Nobody owns this place, except maybe a bank."

"It's OK, Ozzie," I said. I felt sorry for him. He was the perennial little brother to the guys, and he took a lot of flak. He started picking nervously at his face.

"Jason's right," Doug chimed in. "This house is fair game."

"I wonder what kind of person would *want* to stay here," Karendeep said. We all looked at him, surprised he had spoken. He looked back at us, then shook his head as if he hadn't meant to.

"Maybe a bum," said Jason, sounding bored.

"Well, we're the only ones here now," Doug said.

Gently I asked, "Who locked the door?"

Doug went to the windows and examined them, squinting by the light of the small flickering lighter. "Nobody's been out these windows lately," he said.

"Maybe it was just jammed," I said.

"Yeah, that's all it was," Jason said. "This is our place now. The Ravens', OK? From now on we meet here before we go anywhere. Any objections?"

There weren't any. I have to admit Jason was attractive when he acted decisively. I felt that way even knowing that underneath he wasn't sure about anything. Doug had wandered into a big closet and emerged, now wearing a gossamer-thin house slip of some kind. He looked like a large iridescent moth, and he started to shriek and run around the room, fluttering his wings. That set us off.

I found a long black evening dress thoroughly mouthed for years by some of Doug's insect kin. Jason put on a thin pin-striped jacket of a suit and a worn gray felt fedora. Karendeep found an overcoat split up the back to the collar. Ozzie couldn't find anything but a little orange cap that made him look like an organ grinder's monkey, though he tried to make the most of it, jumping about and screeching wildly.

Finally, we fell onto the empty springs of the bed, laughing. It was one of those times I felt very glad to be part of something. Suddenly glad and completely unafraid.

And then, then Jason started to slide his hand up that smelly old dress I had on, trying to grope along the inseam of my jeans. I couldn't believe it. The moon was nailing the bed with a sharp stab of light so the guys could all see. Ozzie was giggling nervously. I froze. Jason's hand crept higher. Ozzie stopped giggling. The room was pulsing with an ugly silence. My mind seemed to rise slowly to the ceiling, where it floated, stiff, terrified. Jason rolled over to kiss me messily on the lips.

I felt as if I were awakening slowly, their faces swimming above me. In a flash my mind returned. I bolted out of the room and down the stairs, half falling in that long black dress. Not so fast, though, that I couldn't hear their immature laughter following me down.

"You trust this John Charles?" Doug was saying.

"Yeah, sure." Ozzie squinted in the clean light. The sun kept glinting like an old man's gold teeth, set high in the tiny windows of the gym. Karendeep was looking at Ozzie's clothes. He had on his chimpanzee's cap, blue T-shirt long enough to brush his knees, and baggy white painter's pants splashed with these electric blue streaks of paint. I approved. A definite skaterhead.

"Nobody knows this guy," Doug continued.

"Since when did we get so choosy?" I said, looking around at everyone. Doug glanced at me, confusion ruining his pretty-boy brow. I liked him best when he was off-balance. I wanted the Ravens to grow, to be something.

"Look, he's a little younger than the rest of us, but he'll do whatever he's told. Honest," Ozzie said.

"At least he's a guy," Doug risked.

I ignored him. If Doug objected to Cat's being a girl and a Raven, that was his problem. "C'mon," I said, pirouetting neatly on my skates and pushing off down the cement walk that ran next to the gym. The Ravens fell in line, and we moved out across the basketball courts and on toward the baseball diamond. Sometimes during the week, after school we used the place to practice tricks. I especially liked to race toward the lunch tables and get some air, graze the top of one of them, and hit the pavement on the other side with some genuine power.

That day I had on new elbow pads and a helmet I'd bought with some cash ol' fatal Bernard had left with Jackie. I headed toward the walkways at the back of the school, knowing it was off-limits to skaters and that anybody in authority still hanging around would nab us. We were thundering alongside the classrooms when I overshot the curbing and plowed into some rosebushes there. The Ravens rolled up and fell around on the grass as if they were drive-by victims and waited for me to recover.

"Good thing you've got that helmet," Doug said. "It's a *real* nice helmet, isn't it, Karendeep? Kind of makes his head look like a Q-Tip." A smile shot across Karendeep's face, then evaporated. I was sizing up Doug. He definitely considered himself second dog, always ready to take over.

Karendeep was looking at his blades. Out of nowhere he says, "My father would like that I not skate. He is not going to buy me any more equipment."

"What? That's nuts!" Ozzie shouted, snorting back some mucus into his throat that he let fly toward the curb, just missing my leg.

"Watch where you're spitting," I said. "Why's that, Karendeep?"

"He wants me to go to school in India. He fears I am losing the old ways."

"That's weird. Hey, at least you'd get out of Whitson," Doug said, his imagination starting to run.

"That why you have those old skates?" I said.

"That is why, yes," Karendeep said solemnly. He said most things that way, a pretty solemn guy all around.

"Here." I unstrapped my helmet and tossed it to him. He looked at me with more gratitude than I wanted, then turned it over in his hands, getting the feel of it. He started to lift it to his head and stopped as it dawned on him and the rest of us, too, that he had his turban to consider. He broke out laughing, and then so did we.

"No, I better not. My father would have me on the fast plane out of here."

"First plane," Doug corrected.

"Yes, first plane. And fast, too. Here." He lifted the helmet. "Thank you, anyway."

"I'll take it," said Ozzie, jumping to his feet.

"Nope," I said, snatching it back. Doug was looking at me curiously.

Karendeep's attention had drifted to the classroom windows. He nudged Doug. I turned to look at what it was they had spied. *It* turned out to be Cat standing in old Mr. Davies's classroom. Davies was there, and clearly he was talking to her very gently 'cause his lips were moving slowly and his eyes were looking at her standing there with her head down, blond hair draped down. I just bet they were talking about me.

"What's up with that?" Doug said.

"Let's get out of here."

"They can't see us," Karendeep said. "The light." He motioned toward the sun beating hot off the windows.

"Ozzie, I think I know what this kid's gotta do if he wants to join up with us," I said.

56

"Got to do? John Charles got to do something?" Ozzie said.

"Yeah. John Charles has got to do something," I replied. "I think we should have him give old Davies a scare." And despite what Karendeep had said, I found I was looking directly at Parker Thurston Davies standing at the window watching me.

19. Sounds

Bid eep baad op ba, bid eep baad dop ba, bid eep, bid eep. Barry was rehearsing with his sax in the living room, and I was in the kitchen policing the flapjack and jam mess from breakfast. I could hear Jackie upstairs, thumping around in the bathroom, readying herself for another day of lying about on a Saturday. Jason was long up and gone. It troubled me that he seemed to spend less and less time around the house once he got over the novelty of living here.

Outside the sink window I watched a pair of blue jays screech and dive-bomb Marcel, our gray tom, who scooted beneath the deck like a ghost ship, quick into port. I listened hard to their squawking and the sad scissoring, scissoring of the sprinklers spewing methodically across the grass, laying down a slow backbeat in time to Barry's riffs. It made me smile to notice how the rhythm fitted neatly, though accidentally. It occurred to me that Barry's music was a kind of hope that the world could fit smoothly together and do what you wanted it to for a change and how, sometimes, the best music can be, by way of some happy accident, a mix of what's outside you and what's inside you, like what I was feeling then.

Yesterday a light rain had fallen, the kind the ground welcomes readily. But I didn't really want to think about yesterday just then. I started to think about Barry's river and the cold, sharp embrace of its wide waters. I let the tap water rush cold over my wrists until I shivered. Jackie says I ought to be careful about telling my feelings to just anybody. She says that when you tell what's in your heart, it can go out of you and into the listener's body and take root in them like Bermuda grass that they can't really ever get rid of. I suppose she should know, what with all the stories men must have told her. But I think that if it didn't work that way, then all anybody would ever be is alone. We'd have nothing to tie us together.

I knew I had Jason hooked in me because my heart had a nest of dry grass woven through it, tight and dying. But I was confused. Earlier that week I'd even tried to talk to Mr. Davies. You know, once Jason took his pocketknife and traced a small half-moon into my wrist until it bled, and then he just looked at me. And after our discovery of the Roost, he took me there alone sometimes. Yesterday . . . yesterday, in that ugly place, he'd kissed me and I let him. I kissed him back and then . . .

I started to imagine Jackie up in her room, drowsing on her bed, letting her eyes drift across the ceiling to the lace curtains rustling softly at the windows. I could see the leaf shadows embroider her face and her skin, still young and delicate. She was trying to decide if it was worth getting up or best to just let the day come to her. She pulled the wet strings of her hair absently through her fingers, put her cool wrists to her forehead like I found myself doing then; she liked that, how it felt simple and good.

Barry stopped playing, and I heard him climb the

stairs, which creaked gently, then the soft collapse of the door closing. I thought of him sliding onto the bed and his fingertips touching her ears still beaded with water from the bath. I liked how Barry was gentle. I could hear someone sobbing softly as if from a distance and realized it was me, and I stopped.

20. Spooked

OK, it *was* punk—getting that funny little kid John Charles to spook old Davies, but being a Raven isn't for free. And I think if you have an idea, it's just smoke unless you make it happen. The problem with most people is they have lots of ideas but no sense of adventure. I tell you, I do, and I have to admit I like that about myself. I like knowing any day I get up might be totally different from the one before just because of what I might do. I'm unpredictable, man. I *like* discovering what's possible. What I didn't like was someone taking an interest in MY CASE. So in a way you could say Davies had it coming to him.

That particular Saturday night Jackie and Cat and Barry were home watching some video about the mob. I was happier to be out with my own little mobsters. And tonight John Charles was going to be my point man. He was a short, stout kid with a bullet-shaped head his dad clippered short every couple of weeks to save on barber bills. He reminded me of those Mexican wrestlers you see on TV. All he would've needed was a close-fitting mask with psychedelic flames around the eyes and some tights, and he would have had the look. The kid was maybe four and a half feet tall, at best, but he had thick arms twisted with the muscles of a man. His eyes held a surprised look that made him seem dumb, though I can't say for sure if he was or not. Can't always tell with little kids.

He was dirt on skates, and that night he kept lagging behind as he and Doug and I scrolled toward the center of town. Ozzie stayed with him, urging him on like an overanxious parent. Davies lived in this prissy little gingerbread house with a sharp, sloping roof and a little castle-looking thing for an entry. It was in a section of nice older homes near the high school that had streets fanned out around it named Yale and Cambridge and Princeton and that kind of drivel. Huge ash trees, with beards of mistletoe, leafed out over the streets, making them cool and dark. Doug was having fun spinning circles around Ozzie and John Charles, nipping at their ears with his fingers as I loped along in front of them, doing a slow, calm, and happy clip, knapsack and cargo strapped to my back. Karendeep moved along quietly, bringing up the rear.

For a moment we stopped at the curb and ogled the place. A little honey-colored light was seeping from the windows through a small stand of birch that were spinning in the breeze. We toed across the lawn and peered right into the front window. And there was Davies sitting on a davenport reading a book, looking like a mannequin in a furniture store's window. No Mrs. Davies as far as we could see. "Look," whispered Doug. And we did.

Next to Davies, just outside the rim of lamplight falling next to him, in the half shadow, there, on the floor, was a thick little man who seemed to be intent on cutting out a huge paper doll from some butcher paper. He had on black trousers that came up above his chubby waist and wide red suspenders. His eyes were strapped in behind these big magnifying kind of glasses. There was

62

something odd about the little man. He had his tongue stuck out, clenched between his front teeth, and he seemed to be concentrating very hard, given completely to the task of cutting a curved line with these oversized scissors. His face was sort of rugged and handsome— short blond hair parted and plastered down neatly. He looked to be maybe in his twenties.

I unfurled my backpack and pulled from it a large plastic bag that I tossed onto the lawn, where it made a thudding sound. "This is your show, Mr. J. Charles."

"Wha-wha-what is it?" he whispered, looking at it as if it might bite.

"It's your chance to join the Ravens." He looked at me, a little hopeless, and I flashed on Baby Saul's face. "Get with it," I snapped.

Ozzie looked over worryingly at John Charles. "OK, c'mon, c'mon," he prompted.

John Charles stooped quickly and grasped the bag and withdrew a large dead crow that Doug had been kind enough to shoot the afternoon before with his .22 from a clump of eucalyptus near the highway. It was a foot or more in length and must have weighed ten pounds, or so it seemed. Someone told me the dead weigh more than the living, though that doesn't seem possible because if a soul weighs something and lightens the load when it leaves, then how come the body isn't lighter? I've wondered if maybe instead of something leaving, it works the other way—that is, that death comes into your body and weighs it some. Maybe it's death fills you and pulls you down.

Anyway, I know that bird was heavy, and stinking to

high heaven, so that John Charles held it high and firmly by its feet, away from him as if it were catching. Its eyes looked sure and dead-on; its feathers caught the light so that for a second they reminded me of Jackie's hair.

Doug and I stayed at the window while John Charles made his way slowly in the dark, carrying his prize upside down, bat fashion, toward the entry, Ozzie tiptoeing behind him. They opened the screen door carefully, placed the bird, then stabbed the bell and dropped back.

Davies's head went up, his eyes to the door, then to the little man. He marked his book and rose and crossed to the door, little man following closely at his shoulder. Huddled, we sank back into the shadows. We heard the door open and the screen door squeak. Davies stepped back into the room, and little man darted forward, past him, Davies trying to grab him but missing. And then little man dropped back behind Davies again, his hands to his ears, his huge insect eyes growing bigger and blinking. He seemed to be screaming, but no sound came.

Jeez. Damn. Man, I tell you, when I got home, I couldn't stop thinking about it. That little man and Mr. Davies—I was starting to feel bad for him, his shot-up face and head, his sorry little life, his poems nobody cared about. I don't like feeling sorry for anybody. It's no use to them. But it got me and I couldn't let it go, so I forced myself to think about something else. Something nice. There was always Cat. Yeah, I could think about her. No one had been around when I got in, just half-empty bowls of popcorn in the living room. I thought of her asleep up-stairs at the other end of the house. I hadn't seen her all day. Probably dreaming something. Pretty Cat.

I started playing back all of yesterday. That dirty rain tapping at the windows. The basement of the Roost. The walls, cold and dark there with the damp. She kissed my chest. Makes me shiver even now.

"Look," I'd said, pointing out the far corner of the room, up where a mass of plumbing was crisscrossed and sagging in the shadows.

"Oh, gosh, Jason, it's a rat!" She squirmed beneath me where we lay on the mattress I'd dragged down there so as nobody would bust in on us upstairs, unexpected. Her legs were smooth and warm under a blanket.

I sat up. "No, calm down. It's a sparrow. Come in through a window, I bet. Yeah, there." I nodded toward one of the panes of glass that looked as though something the size of a fist had punched it.

"Oh, gosh. It *is* a sparrow. It looks like a shy nun with its little black hood, doesn't it?"

"Maybe to you, Cat." I kissed her forehead. She bat-ted her eyelashes at me, smiled. They were shining like wings I've torn from moths. "OK, so you're cute," I reas-sured her. I lay back, and she pressed her mouth into the hollow of my collarbone. "Cat." I twisted to see her. She was listening. I wanted her to listen 'cause what I was go-ing to say was what I was always really thinking. "You don't know . . . how this town makes me feel. Like I can't breathe," I said. "I thought when I got out from under my folks that it would change. You know, feeling trapped with Bernard sitting around, stiff with his whiskey, and Mom with that smile that's just the same as all that cracked china of hers Bernard glues back together."

Cat raised herself on her elbows, her hair dragging my chest. "You wouldn't take off, Jason, would you? Without . . . me?"

I wonder what makes people so helpless. Her eyes were open and big with fear. "No. I wouldn't." It was so easy to say. She wanted me to say it. I felt like saying it. What did it really matter if I didn't know if it was true? She slumped down beside me, play-biting my shoulder. "I want people to look at me and see something special. And that's never going to happen around here."

"Jason, I think you're special."

I smiled and pinched her hip; she squealed and rolled away.

"Seriously, the Ravens think you're special. They're a little afraid of you. But they would do just about anything you said, Jason. And they'd do it because they admire you."

"Afraid? What are they afraid of?"

"Well, your temper for one," she said, trying not to act too careful with me, sitting up, pulling the blanket with her.

"Oh, c'mon. *Everybody* has a temper. That's bull, Cat. That's bull!"

Cat smiled her feline smile. "OK. Just don't take off without me. Promise?"

Those weak eyes again, soft in the darkness of that room. She was making me feel soft inside. Soft and strange, but kind of nice. I rolled over, pulling her down, moving slowly, rocking gently, quietly. She was all darkness and water under me, and I felt a little spooky. I could feel the mattress beneath her and the floor beneath that and the earth under everything, heavy and holding us up. Then that bird started beating and thrashing about the ceiling. Then it settled, 'cause everything was quiet.

21. The Truth

"Hey, sweetheart!"

There was no reason to shout, with him gliding alongside me as I skated. I kept skating and looking ahead as he trolled the cruiser at a fast walk, the door's side mirror almost grazing my elbow. I hated his face, the way he smiled when he looked at me as if I were a bit of candy. You could almost see him smacking his awful lips in his little mind.

"That's a nice hat. I like that. It suits you, you know?"

Officer Moxley was a small man. He was bald and sported a pencil-thin mustache, the kind you might see in a British movie from the thirties. He liked cruising the high school neighborhoods, stopping the girls to quiz them about nothing and show off his cruiser and his German shepherd, Pal.

Pal was barking, and I glanced furtively at the car. Officer Moxley's voice turned suddenly angry, "Shut up!" he commanded. Pal swallowed a whimper and looked away. "The kids call you Cat, am I right?" His voice again, cooing sticky sugar. "Say, why don't you stop and let me talk to you a minute?"

I vowed to myself that I wouldn't, not for any reason.

"You know you have some interesting friends," he continued. He chuckled to himself, his chest rattling, coughing up a morsel of phlegm that seemed to interest him.

I shot him a look that said why-don't-you-find-a-nice-quiet-place-to-hang-yourself, though, in truth, he frightened me.

"I understand you and your friends like to visit your teachers after school," he said, obviously very pleased with himself. "Is that true, Catherine? Do you make house calls?" I glanced at him quickly but couldn't see anything in him but a trace of malice and curiosity. "You know, there's only one little thing that is confusing here? Mr. Davies, now, you know Mr. Davies, don't you, Catherine? He said to let it go. Guess he likes you kids more than I thought. What do you think, Catherine? Why would he do that?"

Then it clicked: Jason begging off that night we watched a gangster flick, the type he *loved*. The Ravens acting oddly around Mr. Davies at school. What had they done now? I braked and swung to face the car. Pal stuck his head out, his tongue lolling spittle onto the door. "Why don't you just leave me alone?" I said sharply.

"Because your boyfriend is trouble and I'm trying to save you some," he shot back. That surprised me because I could tell that he meant it. He could see that he'd gotten to me.

"You might consider making some new friends, Cat. Can I call you that? Cat?"

It's a sick feeling when someone hateful tells you what you already suspect is true.

22. The Law

Around here, sometimes, maybe a cowboy or one of the seasonals who work the motels gets drunk and stabs somebody in one of the dilapidated roadhouses along 395. Couples fight and get out of hand. There's a few regular junkies busy with their small-time burglaries. The usual little-town wanna-be gang bangers do a lot of posing and occasionally take a warning potshot at one another. Plenty of routine stuff for the cops to do, so when they arrested John Charles and Ozzie, it was a true shock to the Ravens.

Ozzie and John Charles, like the brains they were, lit some trash on fire in a Dumpster behind a liquor store near the school a few weeks after we pulled the Davies prank. Officer Moxley, the town cop or cop-of-the-walk, as we called him, was already nosing after us from what Cat said, so he was probably celebrating now. Probably took ol' Mrs. Moxley out to Happy Steak, then home for some legal lovemaking or whatever it is cops do for thrills on their downtime.

Anyway, Ozzie and his new shadow, John Charles, got released to their parents until their court appearance. I called a meeting.

Cat was moody and quiet. She was the first after me and Doug to show at the Roost. It was late in the afternoon. Not much sun made it through the greasy windows, so the house seemed drab. Good ol' Karendeep made it on time and came in the back door, making a lot of noise 'cause he hadn't taken off his skates. He rolled around us slowly for a while in the big living room where we sat on the floor. Nobody said anything.

John Charles never showed. Ozzie chuffed in eventually. He wasn't even on blades. His mom had taken them from him, and he tiptoed in. Doug lit into him without waiting. He surprised even me when he grabbed him by the shirt and held him close to his face. "If you say one word about the Ravens, I'm going to kill you."

He let him go and turned away. Ozzie looked scared but defiant, glaring at Doug.

"When's your court date?" I asked.

"A week, I think. They're supposed to call," he said, looking sullen.

I suppose after the cops and his mom, we were just more of what he'd been up against lately. "What about John Charles?" I asked.

"Same thing. He probably won't get more than a warning, though. They say for me, it's mal—mal-something mischief and arson. At least, that's what they told the old lady."

"Malicious," Cat said.

"What?" Ozzie said.

"Malicious mischief, you little dweeb," Doug added.

"OK. Everybody just shut up. The Ravens had nothing to do with this, and you know it, but it could still bust us up. Everybody keeps away from John Charles from now on. If I get a chance, I'll talk to him. Nobody else. Got it?" I said.

"He already told," Ozzie said, not looking at anybody.

"Told what?" Cat questioned, coming to life.

"Just that he was part of the Ravens and that we were always together and doing stuff," Ozzie replied.

"Stuff?" I just about hollered.

"He doesn't know anything but the prank we pulled on Davies, and nobody would care much about that."

"I want to know why I was never told about what you did to Mr. Davies," Cat said.

"He's your bud, isn't he?" I said, looking her in the eye, questioning, taunting.

"What do you care?"

"*Forget* about that, we've got something to deal with here," Doug said.

"Just leave Mr. Davies alone," she said curtly. "I mean it."

I thought for a moment. "We do as I said. We don't hang together at school anymore. We'll leave it at that."

"Do we have to leave John Charles out?" Ozzie whined.

"Look, Ozzie, John Charles isn't your little toy to play with and boss around," I said.

Karendeep looked at Cat, Cat flashed to Doug, and Doug at me, all of them staring in some kind of disbelief.

"What? What?" I wanted to know.

"Nothing," Cat said.

Karendeep raised his eyebrows and his shoulders like, *yeah, nothing.*

"How come the Ravens never do anything good?" Cat muttered as if to herself.

72

23. Something Special

That first time we took Bobbie fishing I rose early and left the house quietly without awakening anyone. Mr. Davies had given me money, insisting I pack a lunch for dragon slayers, so I went first to the little grocery store that Karendeep's folks ran, situated on a corner downtown. Prices were higher there than at the supermarket out on the strip, but it was more fun to skate downtown with all the side streets and alleys and sidewalks running along the glass windows. I bought sliced ham and cheese, sweet pickles, French rolls and Chee•tos, a handful of chocolate bars, and some hard candy because Mr. Davies said Bobbie liked that especially. I felt very grown up doing the shopping for two guys.

Karendeep loaded up my backpack without saying anything. I kept winking at him every time his mom wasn't looking until finally he broke into a wide, genuine smile. Karendeep was a gentleman. I skated the few quick blocks back to the house and got Bobbie ready to go. A few weeks back Mr. Davies had explained to me that Bobbie had had a very difficult birth, and though many children like him could eventually be independent, Bobbie would always be a child who needed looking after. I was pleased he wanted me to meet Bobbie and to help out with him in my free time. He didn't mention a Mrs. Davies, and I didn't ask. Jackie had been insisting I find a part-time job, anyway, and Mr. Davies said that if things worked out, he could pay me.

73

That day Bobbie put on Levi's, white high-top tennis shoes, and a yellow-and-red Hawaiian print shirt that he left untucked. He looked sharp in his own boxy way. Bobbie never looked me in the eye the first few weeks that I knew him. I could tell he was very interested in me because he would always hang close by, but most of the time his eyes would gaze through his glasses, out somewhere past my left ear. A shy puppy.

It was a warm, sweet day, with white, puffy clouds drifting by effortlessly, the first warmth teasing a few trees into leaf. We took Mr. Davies's van, Bobbie sitting in the back by himself, methodically counting the houses on the blocks of the old neighborhoods. We drove out of town and down to the river to park the van and take a path beaten between the cattails to the water. Bobbie could bait his own hooks, though he winced as he pushed them through the tubular bodies of the earthworms he plucked from a coffee can. Mr. Davies didn't fish; he seemed to enjoy watching Bobbie and the river and the willows and the cottonwoods there.

I read a book I had with me all about the old houses of England. I tried imagining a great stone house out at the bend of the river where the water slid around, digging in its heel and pulling thin walls of orange dirt into itself. We ate all we could of the food, with Bobbie, orange Chee•tos dust smeared around his lips, polishing off the entire jar of pickles. Mr. Davies pointed out how Bobbie mimicked the way I ate my sandwich, all the edges first before munching the center. We laughed and Bobbie laughed, also, and he knew what the joke was, too.

That Mr. Davies was lonely I could see plain enough.

His very face was a kind of distance, though he wasn't the type to make a show of it. Sitting by the water, he looked like a castle bricked up for years, though, now, crumbling a bit. His sweater was rumpled, and his pants needed ironing. I didn't know that I was lonely, too, until I sat there with him admiring the sun on the water. He looked at me and smiled. We watched a sand crane catapult off a bluff on the far bank, lift, and work its way past where maples flamed above the cold green water.

"How old were you when you went to England?" I asked, almost an afterthought to all I was thinking. He had mentioned it in class a few times.

"Oh, my early twenties. After the war. I wasn't there more than five days. Expensive place for a kid. Well, for anybody."

"It wasn't a disappointment, was it?"

"Oh, no. London's everything and more than you imagine, Cathy. It was just I wasn't in the best frame of mind at the time. I do know what the inside of a pub looks like, though." He chuckled to himself.

"I just *know* it will change me," I said. "I know if I can only get there, everything will change."

He glanced at me, shook his head slowly. "Change is an inside job, Cathy. It happens in your heart," he said, his voice gentle. He started pulling chunks of grass and tossing them into the wind, watching after them.

"But I'll end up like Jackie if I stay here," I protested. Couldn't he understand that? I knew he could. He was the most understanding person I knew.

"Your mom may have done all right. Do you know how little she had to start with?"

"Did you know my mom when you were . . . young?" I asked, surprised.

"Only in the way everyone in a small town thinks he knows everyone, I guess."

"What was she like?"

"I think she had a rough time. I didn't really know her. I was already teaching when she came through Emerson. She was never my student, though. I think she had a tough time, that's all."

"Oh . . . But *you* got out. *You* went away."

"Yes, I did—Marines, then college. But I took myself with me wherever I went."

"What do you mean?"

He turned slowly to face me and took me by the shoulders. "Listen." He paused. "You keep that dream of yours. It's a fine one. And you very well may be right. It might change everything." He pulled his hands away and seemed to be thinking with purpose, his eyes blinking rhythmically. "Let me give it some thought, Cathy. It could be that I can help."

I felt then as close to Mr. Davies as I had to anyone, ever. Maybe that's what telling your dream to the right person does. I think that's so.

It was a long, dreamy day. Bobbie caught seven tiny bluegills and a whitefish of respectable proportion, all of which he threw back after examining them closely, rubbing his fingers back and forth quickly over the slick, fleshy skin as if with a secret and special blessing of his own making.

24. Waiting

I was kicking it on the floor of my room, breeze coming through the back door. In March, in the valley up along the eastern slope of the Sierras, the temperature climbs into the seventies, and it's comfortable. Cat would say dreamy. It was Saturday, she was gone again, and Barry had taken Jackie to a matinee.

I thumbed through the phone book, found the number I was after, and dialed. "Whitson County Juvenile Detention Center," said the clipped voice on the other end.

"Yes, my name is Gerald Lockwood. May I speak with my son?"

"Your son?"

"Yes, Ozzie—Osborne Lockwood," I managed to say.

"Is he an employee or a ward of the court?"

"Ward?" I said, puzzled. "Well, he's locked up."

"I'm sorry, sir, I can't call a ward to the phone. Visiting hours are between three and six P.M., though you'll have to make an appointment in advance. Would you like me to transfer you to someone who can help you with that?"

I hung up. I called Karendeep's house and let it ring for a long time before someone answered. It was a woman who sounded proud and kind of demanding. I hung up. Thought about it and dialed again.

"Hello. Hello. To whom am I speaking?" the voice said.

"Hello, this is Jason, is Karendeep there? I mean, could he come to the phone?"

Long pause. I could tell she was thinking. "One moment, please," she said flatly.

"Hello, this is Karendeep." His voice sounded deep and adult.

"Hey, Karendeep. Hey, what say we go visit Ozzie?"

"No. I am not able to go out today. Thank you very much. I will call you. Good-bye." That was that. I got the picture.

I was wondering where Cat was when I heard Barry's car rumble into the driveway. Car doors slammed. Barry passed my window, walking stiffly toward the garage out back, and seconds later Jackie came by. She was in a hurry.

"So what exactly does that mean?" she was saying, her voice sort of shrill.

I couldn't see Barry from any of the windows or the back door of my room that opened to the yard. His voice came from the shadow of the garage door he had opened. "Damn it, Jackie, I'm here all the time, anyway! Don't you want me to *want* to be here?"

"That's not the point."

"It's your world, Jackie." The voice came clear and low from the dark. Jackie had one hand on her hip and her head thrown back.

Suddenly she whipped around and marched toward the house, her head down. I stepped away from the door.

I busied myself with my little TV, switching the dial and wedging the antenna around. The screen door slammed, and I turned. Jackie's eyes snapped over me, and she stopped and then smiled weakly. "Hi, lover boy." She seemed confused. "Where's Cat?"

"I dunno," I said.

She crossed the room to the door leading into the main house. "Do you care?" she asked, looking deeply into my eyes.

"Sure." I shrugged.

She was squinting at me. "You say that like a man." I knew she wasn't giving me a compliment, but I wanted very much to tell her that she could talk to me if she wanted, that I wouldn't get the wrong idea or anything, though I guess I did want to touch her, touch her hair maybe, just once, to run my fingers through it. Jackie was the kind of person that was so much her own self it was natural to feel an attraction to her. I had this odd feeling she was reading my mind because she frowned and said, "Cat's crow," then left the room, and I felt sour, like a kid again.

25. Keeping House

I pressed my belly to the sink, leaning in to scrub the bottom of a pot that Mr. Davies must have burned something in at one time. The place was a mess, and I was enjoying putting things right. I was coming by regularly after school for a couple of hours to do wash, pack a lunch for Bobbie to take with him to school the following day, and straighten up the kitchen. Mr. Davies said it was just enough to give him some breathing room and time to grade papers.

Bobbie sat at the table and conversed in a low gurgle with Alfred, his guinea pig, who sat in his lap, trembling. He had just come in from cutting the lawn. It was nowhere near summer, and the Bermuda grass didn't need it, but Bobbie didn't care. Last year he had learned how to use the big trimmer mower they had, and he would've cut the grass every day if he could've. He'd been waiting all winter, and finally Mr. Davies had said that he could go to it today if he liked. Mr. Davies thought this summer if their own yard wouldn't satisfy him he might turn him loose on the neighbors' lawns.

Mr. Davies wandered into the kitchen and sat down, straddling a chair backward, tilting his head at Bobbie the way dogs do when curious. "How's Alfred?" Bobbie giggled. "Don't forget to put him back in his cage, OK, sport?" Mr. Davies said.

"OK," Bobbie answered. His voice always sounded deeper than I expected it to.

"You can stay for dinner if you like, Catherine. I'm making my world-famous spaghetti."

"I hope you're not talking about the couple of hundred cans of SpaghettiOs I found in the cupboards," I teased.

"No." Mr. Davies chuckled to himself. "Sport there had a passion for those things a couple of years ago. He won't touch them anymore."

"Oh, glad you told me. I was thinking of warming some up for him sometime."

"Well, I daresay Bobbie would eat about anything you gave him. He's pretty keen on you, you know." Bobbie was listening with pleasure and a little embarrassment.

"I can't stay for dinner." I could, of course. Jackie was working, and Jason usually made sandwiches for himself. I wanted to stay, but I thought Mr. Davies asked out of politeness. He was very polite. I didn't want them to get tired of me, and so I regulated my stays to the agreed two hours for which I was hired.

"Sure? Well, I'll save you some meatballs. You can try them tomorrow. Hey, Cathy, do you know how to play chess?" he asked suddenly.

I'd seen the board set up in the living room the first time I was over. It had these intricate medieval warriors cast in bronze or something, very impressive. "No. You going to teach me?" I asked.

"Say the word."

"Sometime, yes, sure. Bobbie's lunch is in the fridge, and these dishes are about done."

"I can't tell you how nice it is that you are . . . helping out," he stammered.

It was odd to see Mr. Davies stuck on his words. It gave me a satisfaction I didn't understand.

26. "Juvie"

I dunno, I guess I was expecting glass partitions, guards with M-16s and so on. But the room where I met Ozzie had the simple no-nonsense look of a church basement— cement block walls with a couple of TVs bolted to them, fluorescent lights, high windows. There were about twenty people scattered about at the tables, visiting the kids that were guests of the county. The only way I could get in to see him was by posing as his brother. Only family were allowed visits. I eased in the door sideways and watched Ozzie walk to a table, looking around to see who his visitor was. He looked different—bent and cautious. He saw me and smiled and waved me over to the table, a large blue fiberglass-looking thing. He had on an orange jumpsuit, like an undersized mechanic.

We shook hands, which was strange, as we'd never done that before. I fished in my pocket for the pack of smokes I'd brought and tossed them on the table.

"Thanks, but I quit," he said. "Somebody would only get after me and take them, anyway. But thanks."

He'd been in a week, and I knew he'd be out pretty soon, but I wanted to see him. I'm not saying we were that close, but he was a Raven, and besides, I was curious. "Cat says hi," I said.

"How's she doing? How's the guys?" he asked in reflex, without much interest.

"Everybody's good. Haven't seen John Charles, except in the halls at school."

"That's natural."

"Damn, Ozzie, some of these characters look pretty scary." I was watching a guy with pale pit-bull eyes and barbed wire tats on his neck talking to his mother at the next table. Ozzie forced a half smile and nodded in agreement. "Don't worry, you'll be out of here soon, and we'll get out and do some real skating," I reminded him.

"I've got some time after here when I have to wear this electronic monitor. I can only go to school and then home," he said dryly.

"Oh." I was starting to wish I hadn't come.

"My dad's back in town. Says he may get a job trucking closer to home."

"That sounds like a drag," I said, thinking of Bernard.

"I love my dad," he said quickly, then: "Well, he's OK." Embarrassed he'd said it.

"You can love your ol' man if you want, Ozzie."

"Yeah, sure, hey, the old lady wigged out, you know. Went back to church. She'll probably give up *Jeopardy!* for Lent." We both smiled. Then he leaned forward. "Ishmael's in here. Been here for a while now. That's why you haven't seen him around."

"What?"

"Got ninety days and I don't know what else, for stealing a car or cars, I don't know exactly. Second offense."

"No kidding?"

"He's asking about you."

"Me?"

"Yep." He lowered his voice. "Says he hears you know something about his little brother, Baby Saul."

I looked away. "That's crazy," I said, then gently, carefully: "What did you tell him?"

"Haven't talked to him. He's in a different barrack. Just heard it."

My mind raced, shuffling through snapshots of Doug's sullen face, Ishmael driving by, glowering from his Impala, the dark red blood circling Baby Saul's head.

Ozzie was squinting at me, the sound of his voice coming from a long way off: "Jason, what happened that night?"

"You were there. The cops came and we jetted out," I said, feeling almost drunk and sick.

"Yeah, but we scattered. I only know that me and Doug and Karendeep cut back toward Main and hopped a bus out to the ballfield behind school."

"I've told you before. I skated around till I found you guys. That's it."

"Well, somebody slammed into that kid near St. Peter's the same night we snagged all that audio gear, and Ishmael knows the Ravens sold that stuff."

"Doug sold the stuff," I muttered.

"You sure you don't want to talk to Ishmael? You used to be pretty tight, you know," he reminded me.

"No. I do not want to talk to Ishmael. I haven't got anything to say."

"You know, I've still got some time to go in here," he said, looking at me squarely, his green eyes drilling me. I felt clammy. I wanted out of there. I was glad I wasn't Ozzie. He started to tear up a little, and I realized he was still pretty much a kid.

He slid the pack of cigarettes from the table into his pocket. "I can trade them," he explained, sniffling a little.

"Good. Well, there's nothing to worry about," I lied.

27. Full Moon

I skated down Poplar all the way to Eighth, where the railroad tracks crossed before they tacked out along the river past the town's boxed light, all the way, I knew, out to the mesa and beyond, down to Tucker City and further. A girl out past midnight is foolish, maybe not in her right mind. Cold at that hour, the streets are hushed and waiting, and dogs bark, solitary in the distance. I took the middle of the street because why not? They were mine, alone. In some places the streetlights were out, and those blocks were dumb faith. I might as well have been blind except for the moon, old and swollen, arcing the patch of black above me. I tried to tell myself there was no reason to panic, but tears bit my eyes.

I took the frontage road at Peach and skirted a dead orchard of stumps that ran for a quarter of a mile or more until I could smell it: the bitter smell of sour grass blowing up from the river. I was thinking of my sister and wondering what she thought of me.

When I came to the cottonwoods lining a gravel parking lot where I knew lovers parked in summer, I took off my skates and picked my way down to the water. I knew the river was there because I could feel the cold dampness rising off its surface settling on my face and my arms. Breathless and cramping from exertion, I put my hand to my belly, though nothing was there that I could feel, just my whole life sliding through me, silent, just the snuffling of water against a bank of wet grass that I knew, even then, I would recall for as long as I lived.

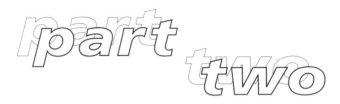

part two

"I've never seen the ocean," Cat said wistfully. Bingo, I thought. I had her now.

"That's right, if we *don't* go, we're crazy!" I nearly shouted.

"Jason, by road Santa Cruz is over five hundred miles," Karendeep said.

"So what's a few hours?" It was early evening, and we were in the Roost.

Doug's ears pricked up. "The coast." He rolled the word around in his mouth like a tasty gumdrop. "The coast. Yeah! Whoa! Why not!" Then his face folded. "Jason, you've got maybe seven hours each way. That's if we're lucky. *If* we get rides regularly, which we won't. Doesn't that mean we've got to spend one night there? Heck, even then we're only there a few hours."

"That's long enough for me. C'mon, guys, just think about it. These are national skaters. We are talking a premier in-line skate exhibition! Ramps, walls, rails, the best skaters in the country."

Cat was looking torn, her eyes full of concern. Then she perked up. "You know, Jason. Barry might take us if we asked him."

"No! Nobody asks anyone! Look, Barry *might* do it, but then we've got to get Jackie to give the OK, and what are the chances Karendeep's or Doug's folks are going to say yes, too? Or let's say Barry changes his mind. And what about the school?"

"Sooooo we just go and face the music when we get back?" Doug asked.

"I don't even know what my folks would do to me. It would be very bad, though," said Karendeep.

"Yeah, you're not even living at home, Jason. Easy for you to talk," Doug added.

"Guys, listen." I paused, closed my eyes, and said slowly, "All anybody does in this town is watch TV and then drive over to the mall to buy the junk they see on TV and then back home for more TV! This is a chance to live a little, don't you *see* that?"

"I do more than that." Cat was offended.

"OK, you do, but that's not really the point," I said. "The point is to make our own excitement."

"God, to really get *out* of here. We'd need some cash, tickets, food, motel, you know," Doug said, sounding a little excited, still dreaming, I knew, but on the right track.

"Yeah, but not much. Tickets for the show, yes, but we don't eat a lot, and we can sleep on the beach. There's miles of them." I knew this to be true because my folks and I spent a week every summer in Santa Cruz. It was a coastal resort, and I'd seen lots of people sleeping on the beach. They were posted—no visitors after midnight—but there were too many miles of them for the cops to patrol, and so people did it all the time.

"What if we don't get rides or somebody sees us on the road and calls the cops?" Doug asked.

"So they do. Trip's over. But they *won't*."

"It would sure be something to remember," he said.

"That's what I'm afraid of," Karendeep said.

"I guess Ozzie misses this one," Cat mused.

"Nobody told Ozzie to start burning up trash cans," I snapped. "What say we take a vote?" I raised my hand and smiled all around.

Doug looked at me hard. "If Jason's going, I'm going." Then his eyes lit up, and he let loose that smile of his. Cat shook her head and smiled, too, then raised her hand. We all looked at Karendeep.

"We'll be *legends*, man," I said.

He looked at me. "I am thinking, that is exactly what would be the problem." But his hand went up.

29. Dinner

Bobbie sat in a large, overstuffed chair in the living room, a big book in his hands, his eyes scouring the pages slowly as he murmured to himself, rocking forward and back, keeping time with some invisible drummer. His hands were large and masculine like his father's. "I didn't know he could read," I said to Mr. Davies. We were into a game of chess that I was losing, though I suspected Mr. Davies was prolonging things so as not to discourage me.

He glanced at Bobbie. "He can . . . a little. He likes to read the same things over. He'll do that for hours sometimes. But, tonight, he's mostly keeping an eye on us."

Mr. Davies had fried squid with onions for dinner. They were kind of rubbery but tasted OK. I was surprised he could cook and seemed at home in the kitchen. I was thinking about that when I asked, "Did you learn to cook after Mrs. Davies left?" It just came out, and when his head snapped up and his eyes narrowed, I felt like a fool for having said it.

Fatigue seemed to sweep over his face, and he shrugged. "No. I could always cook." His eyes went back to the board. A long silence, then: "I was difficult to live with after the war. And Bobbie, Bobbie was a shock, you know . . . some people aren't built to handle things very well. Not their fault. It's just their nature. Ann, my ex, lives in Topeka with her sister."

94

He seemed calm, and what he said, ground he'd been over many times before. A siren pierced the silence from a distance. The front door was open, and the jasmine, just blooming, drifted in with a breeze. Ann. When he said her name, she was, for a second, almost real to me. And he, Mr. Davies, seemed more real to me, too. I realized he was more to me than a teacher.

I asked him, "Do you ever get scared? I mean, really frightened?" I blushed then and felt like a geek.

He looked at me, his face drawing tight. "Sure."

"Why is that, I mean, that everybody seems scared of something?"

"Keeps you alive, I guess."

"Oh, I don't mean scared of running into the street when a bus is coming or anything. Of course, you've got to be afraid of some things. I mean, well, scared of the things that might be just what you needed." Mr. Davies studied the board and didn't say anything. I said gently, "Like right now, you're afraid you might say something that would hurt me." Immediately I wished I hadn't said it. I winced inwardly.

His eyes stayed with the board. He sighed and shook his head. "No. I was thinking of Nam, how the fear was so constant there that you had to learn to deal with it. Like a bad friend that you don't have the nerve to shake. The only thing to do was to accept it and learn to focus on the task in front of you. But you could never forget it. Get killed if you did."

I was glad for his fear and that it had kept him alive and that I was sitting there talking to him. I moved my last pawn uncertainly. "My mom's afraid. Afraid of the

95

one guy I think might treat her decently, if she'd let him. And I think he messes around to protect himself, so he won't get hurt if she dumps him."

"Be careful about judging folks, Catherine. They might know things about themselves you don't."

"Like what?"

"Like maybe they've followed a road you haven't and they know the danger."

"But you're going to get hurt by something sometime, anyway. Why put yourself into a box on purpose?"

"What are you afraid of, Catherine?"

I didn't want to answer that, not even to myself. He had me, though, after all my big talk. I felt suddenly self-conscious and awkward. "Well, a lot of stuff, but I'm . . . not completely sure talking about it will help," I said.

"And it might hurt, too." He looked over at Bobbie, who was now in the corner of the room staring at a daddy longlegs that was setting up house on the ceiling. He spoke softly, carefully. "I'm scared of what might happen to Bobbie when I'm gone. It makes me sick even to think of it. Maybe that's the worst thing: loving somebody and being afraid for him. Knowing you don't have the power to save him."

I looked at Bobbie, and suddenly I could see him as Mr. Davies did: perhaps only temporarily protected and safe.

"I guess you're right, Catherine. You've got to face it, whatever it is," he muttered. He picked up the rook, reconsidered in midair, and returned it, puzzling over his move some more.

"Even if you know it will scare the one you love, if you tell them?"

"Tell them what?" His head snapped up. "You need to tell somebody something, Catherine?" He looked very nervous at this, started fidgeting with the buttons on his shirt, and I realized, as my heart kicked, he thought I had something to tell *him*.

30. Breaking Free

It was cold. Cat and I had jackets, but at 4:00 A.M., with light in the east scarcely nudging the horizon and a wind coming in off the hills, they couldn't keep us from shivering. I remember the red stalks of a couple of radio towers in the distance and crossing a deserted car lot, with its string of lightbulbs there, still glowing in the half dark, rattling in the wind. For the first time I wondered if I was wrong about the fun we would have.

Karendeep had backed out at the last minute, saying his folks needed him at their business, but he'd pirated some snacks from the store, and we had them in our packs. Cat left a note for Jackie telling her we hadn't run away or anything and not to worry. She said we'd gone out along the river to camp and talk some things out and that we'd be back in a couple of days. I can't fault her for that. We didn't want the highway patrol after us or anything.

I'd made some money, though not much, hauling trash with Jackie's landlord. Karendeep gave me a little. Finally, I'd gone around to see Bernard, hinted I was low on cash, and he came across with a few bills he stuffed in my shirt pocket along with the usual useless advice about staying calm and taking things easy. Cat had the money she'd made taking care of Davies's little man, and Doug had made some washing car windows over at the parking lot at the mall.

We sat out on the highway and waited a full hour before Doug showed, looking cold, a little scared, but smiling. Doug was a punk, but because he hadn't backed out on us, I know it lifted our spirits to see him. Our first ride came quickly, a rancher hauling his own chickens down 395, and we sat, all three of us, squeezed in the passenger's seat. It was this big black throne that Doug and I fitted into easily, Cat sitting on my lap, her head almost bumping the window. The driver went on in god-awful detail about three-day hauls and how chickens get stressed by the trip. He certainly had a three-day stink going, and his eyes had some kind of desert light pouring through them. I think he was speeding on something, but hell, he was friendly and asked almost nothing about ourselves. We just said that we were going to L.A. to see Cat's aunt. We suffered through three hours of the perils of the chicken business.

In Mojave he dropped us near a doughnut shop, where we scarfed down some pastry and coffee, watching the before-work crowd slip in and out. Hyped up, shaky on our nerve, sugar, and caffeine, our mouths running about our obvious charm and how easy this whole thing was going to be, we walked back to the highway and stood around watching the traffic zoom past us. Doug tossed pebbles at me, trying to aggravate me, though pretending he was kidding around. I ignored him.

It got warm in a hurry, so we shed our coats to take turns holding a thumb out. We started getting goofy and cracking stupid jokes out of boredom. Finally an old Ford van pulled over, and the guy driving, a salesman of some kind with one front tooth capped in silver, said he had room for one, and Cat could come along if she liked. As if we were that stupid. I just shook my head, and he pulled away, but it was chilling to have that happen, and we fell silent.

Though still warm, the weather began to stack up. Headlights winked on, and rain came, cutting hard at an angle, Cat frowning at me as if it were my fault. Just then a big rig, lit up like Christmas, its load whipped with a loose canvas, shunted its brakes down and came hissing to a stop. When we climbed up to the height of the driver with his big grin, his big beard runny with chew, I believed myself, just then, pretty lucky to be fifteen, moving west with the clouds.

But feeling safe is never a sure thing, and it was only a couple of minutes before I wasn't so sure. "He's drunk," I whispered to Cat. I'd caught how his eyes looked pale and far away like Bernard's, and his tongue was heavy when he spoke. He definitely was flooring that rig, though it seemed only to inch up the ankles of the Tehachapis. He wasn't exactly shy, either. We got the life story—a hitch in the Navy, oil rigs in the Gulf of Mexico, and prefabbing mobile homes in a factory outside Baton Rouge, Louisiana. Now he pulled short hauls out of Bakersfield. He kept rolling his eyes over Cat's body, but he was so pitiful it didn't really bother me.

We crested the pass and started the long, dangerous slide toward the valley, the truck really picking up speed, the trailers in back wagging dangerously. Doug was tight with fear, and Cat had her eyes closed and looked as if she might be praying. The guy glanced at them and started laughing, spitting into a Styrofoam cup he had in one hand and taking long, thirsty pulls from a pint he pulled from under his seat with the other. I noticed his Adam's apple bouncing appreciatively when he swallowed. With his hands occupied with bottle and cup, only his palms free to steady the wheel, the rig began a slow drift toward the next lane and a pint-sized Dodge convertible.

Right then I stopped enjoying Cat and Doug's terror and kind of panicked myself. I reached out and grabbed the wheel and pulled on it gently. The truck seemed to list for a second, then pulled a plumb line. In the mirror I caught the driver of the convertible stabbing a finger skyward.

Suddenly awake, he roared, "Kid, I'll do the driving!"

"Yeah, sure," I muttered. But I was pissed that he'd scared me. He clammed up after that. I didn't care. We rode on in silence. Cat snuggled into me.

When finally Doug spotted what he said was the Kern River in the distance, twisting into the toy trees and houses of Bakersfield, I was holding Cat, and it occurred to me that I liked her like this; she was cute when she was really scared.

31. Grace

I said a prayer of relief, a snippet flaring upward, *Thank God*. What a relief to be sitting in the shade of a mulberry on the side of the road outside Bakersfield, free of that awful driver and the torture he'd given us. Hitchhiking wasn't very romantic. Jason was busy passing out snacks Karendeep had given him—beef jerky, little crackers with cheese, peanuts. Doug was munching rapidly, his hair pushed askew in the wind.

"Here," Jason said, passing me a warm bottle of Dr Pepper he brought from his pack.

I smiled at him. He smiled back broadly. I blinked; I was sleepy now that the adrenaline was draining out of me. I hadn't slept properly in the days before the trip, and the world seemed somewhat blurry. Jason seemed odd and frenetic, rifling through his pack, winking, and smiling. But he was being very protective and polite, and I could tell he was having fun, his eyes sparkling in the way that I loved.

Eventually we got a ride from a couple of farmworkers up from Mexico, driving an old car with loads of room for us in the backseat. They spoke just a little English and looked rough, covered in a fine powdery dust that they managed to explain, when asked by Doug, was some sort of pesticide. Apparently crop dusters sometimes overshot their mark and caught anybody still out in the fields. They'd been working a mammoth orchard of almonds outside Oildale and taken a direct hit the day before and hadn't had a place to shower. One of them kept zooming his hand and making a *shshsh*ing sound to show how it happened.

They kept sneaking looks at us in the rearview mirror and occasionally spoke rapidly in a fine melodic Spanish. Doug decided they needed to know what he knew about the Central Valley and its history, so we all got to hear one of his lectures. The valley was a savanna by nature, like the Serengeti of Africa, until settlers from Europe dug the first canals from the rivers to irrigate. Then in the thirties the government dammed the rivers and constructed huge canals, and big-business farms sprang up to commandeer the water. Most of the work in the fields had been done by huge waves of immigrants, mostly Oklahomans out of the Dust Bowl and laborers up from Mexico, and so on and on . . .

If Doug didn't always look so pleased with himself when he spoke, finding out some of that stuff might have been tolerable to Jason, I think. He was obviously irritated, clenching his teeth, feigning sleep. I doubted our driver and his friend understood much of it, though they nodded and smiled. All those miles and monotonous rows of lettuce and alfalfa, cotton and corn, pistachios, figs, and who-knows-what quickly lost their wonder and made me drowsy.

It was a couple of hours before our friends dropped us abruptly in Los Banos and drove off in a swirl of dust to jobs they had waiting on a ranch working vines. We were stranded until about four in the afternoon, when Jason hatched a plan to let me thumb the ride while Doug and he hid behind some oleanders growing in the heat by the side of the road. I was not very sure about the guys leaving me out there by myself and was asking myself just how stupid was I when, sure enough, an out-of-work plumber in an ancient VeeDub van painted shocking pink pulled over. I opened the passenger door, hesitating while the guys sprang from the bushes and hopped in behind me. The driver crushed the stick shift into first gear and shook his head angrily, though he said nothing.

To our driver Jason nodded, saying dryly, "Thanks." Then he took my hand and squeezed it, and I was suddenly glad.

That old, old buggy really strained up the coastal range through a long slash of a road that was the pass out of the valley. I held Cat's hand all the way over even though it was sweaty and warm. I figured she was on the verge of complaining about our using her as bait to get a ride, and I didn't want her chickening out now we were well on our way.

The wind kicked up, every once in a while broadsiding us in gusts, sending the van veering into the next lane. The plumber who gave us the ride was a little unhappy about being tricked, I think, but he didn't give us any trouble. But when we hit Hollister, a little farm and cattle town just the other side of the mountains that reminded me of home, he dumped us, quick enough, complete with some weak-ass admonition to Doug and me about getting ourselves into trouble traveling around with a little girl.

In Hollister we were standing on the strip, trying to decide if we should spend some cash and get something to eat or just push on, when a cop car trolled past us very slowly, the patrolman giving us the once-over. When he pulled over and swung a U, we shot into a café. I sat at the counter, and Doug took a booth in the rear. Cat hit the john and stayed there. He pulled past the front window, craning his neck, but must not have seen us because he drove on. I knocked at the door to the ladies' room, and Cat came out, looking nervous.

"Where did he go?" she asked.

"Who? The cop?"

"Yes." A plea in her voice.

"Cops aren't that big a deal, Cat," I told her.

"They'd be a big deal to Jackie."

"Forget it." I held her in my eyes, speaking gently. "Are you with me, Cat? Are you?"

Her face gave up slowly. "Yes, I'm with you."

"Good." I smiled. That was easy enough.

We ended up feasting on fried chicken, string beans, and mashed potatoes, and Doug left the waitress, a redhead with bad teeth who called each of us sweetie, a five-buck tip, which was just plain showing off if you ask me.

It was getting late, and we didn't know where we'd sleep if it wasn't the beach, so we hustled out of the place, and Cat did her thumbing solo while Doug and I lounged on a bus bench. A bashed-up turquoise blue Ford Bronco with a couple of orange surfboards strapped to the luggage rack on top pulled over, and that's how we met Tommie and Alex. The last thing I remember was the sun getting sleepy on a ridge of oak and black cattle, and dropping my head into Cat's lap, drifting off to the hum of the motor, her watching me with some kind of goofy, fatal affection.

33. The Beach

It was dark when Tommie turned off Highway 1 and onto the streets of Santa Cruz. Doug had finally exhausted himself with questions about surfing and was, like Jason, dead to the world. Alex was cute, with sun-bleached reddish hair, a tan, and a compact body of muscles that rippled beneath his T-shirt. Tommie was tall and gangly, with a torch of very black hair that rose off his head in haphazard fashion. He had deep green eyes that glanced at me shyly. I wondered what they thought of a girl who was out driving around with a bunch of guys at night. They were both seniors at the high school in Hollister. They were cutting school the next day. The waves were supposed to be good right then, and they wanted a full day of surfing and so had set out late in the afternoon after classes.

We stole through the darkened streets toward the ocean. We had the windows down and could feel its moisture already. It made me feel light and expectant. Tommie took a hard right and drove down an abrupt side street that ended in a cul-de-sac edging the cliffs and parked. We sat there for a moment listening to the sea's heavy breathing.

Doug and Jason, pulled out of their sleep by the absence of the motor's running, sprang out of the truck and started whooping and hollering. I climbed out slowly, legs stiff and unresponsive.

Alex leaned out of his window. "Hey, keep it down,"

he growled. "You're going to attract attention and blow it." The guys stopped their celebrating, looking chastised and foolish. They seemed to accept that Alex and Tommie were older and knew what was what. We grabbed our gear, Alex and Tommie taking care to unload their boards, and clambered over the cliff's edge, following them. No moon yet; dark. I was glad of our guides because on our own this would have been chancy. They knew the way, and in short order, we found ourselves on the sand. It felt warm between my toes and on the soles of my feet when I took off my sandals. It was finer than the sand on the little strips around the river back in Whitson.

We tramped out to within thirty yards of the water and threw down our stuff. The boys set about gathering driftwood, the drier pieces near the cliffs, to start a fire. Alex went back to the truck and returned with some hot dogs he'd stored in a cooler. We roasted them on sticks, then wrapped them in slices of bread to eat, standing in a circle, our shadows twitching like pagans around us. The food tasted the way all food does in the outdoors—delicious, almost holy.

Stuffed, we lay back on our blankets, and for the first time that long day I felt the fear drain out of me. The guys exchanged stories about surfing and skating while I let myself sink into the sand, which was still giving off a faint heat from the day's sun. Slowly, persistently, worry crept back into me, through my stomach and up into my chest, where it rested. I wondered if this was the freedom that Jackie was always talking about.

34. The Secret

I woke before dawn and sat up in my blankets. Cat stirred, but I was careful not to wake her. I reached over and tapped Doug until one eye of his woke and stared at me as if questioning who I was. I motioned to him that we should go for a swim. He nodded in agreement, though sleepily. Standing, I saw the waves out there gray and rolling their muscles. The sun was cracking under a stack of clouds on the horizon that reminded me of a bunch of blue shop rags. A breeze blowing, kicking up whitecaps. I got up, shucked the sand from my hair, and started racing toward the water. I heard the thump, thump, thump of Doug's feet hitting the sand behind me. As we neared the water, the surf sounded a deep rumbling. We dived.

The water was so cold my heart leaped, shocked into action. I cleared the wave, entering the depth behind it. I surfaced, swimming hard, with just enough power to crest the next incoming swell. Then a large wave slapped me back into myself, sending me tumbling, spit back onto the shore, my arms scraped, my chin warm with blood, I guessed. I stood up, letting the water pull at my ankles, and smiled.

Doug was out about twenty-five yards, treading water, shouting, his voice snatched by the wind so I could scarcely hear him. I waded out a few feet, jumping the first wave to hit me, and then swam out to meet him. We slapped the water, moving slowly in circles. I grabbed his head and pulled him under. He kicked me, and I released him, both of us laughing and sputtering water. Finally, we headed in, awake and satisfied for the moment. I felt calm. Spent.

When we returned to our little camp, Cat and the guys were awake, Tommie and Alex suiting up in these trick black wet suits. They were eager to go and were quietly exchanging quick estimations to each other regarding the look of the surf. I was wishing we had the time to spare to have a go at it, too, but we didn't, and I knew, anyhow, they wanted to surf, not teach us how.

Doug was walking them down to the water, quizzing them again. I could hear him back home spouting off on the details of the sport. Cat was sitting, hugging her knees and staring off into the distance. I fell next to her, scattering wet sand. "You're not going in, are you," I stated.

"No."

"You're maybe missing the best part of the trip, you know."

"No. I'm enjoying the best part." She looked at me and tousled my hair. "You're wet! Ugh." She laughed. Cat was pretty. I liked to just look at her sometimes, just shut off my head and admire her blue eyes, yellow hair, the little freckles that dotted her cheeks that had gone shrimp pink from standing out in the sun most of yesterday.

"How come you never go in?" I asked.

"I've told you a hundred times it gives me the willies," she said offhandedly.

"Yeah, but you never say *why*. You know, Jackie told me you know how to swim. Whatever the reason, it's not good enough. You should never just quit."

"Well, I have."

"Whatever." I let my eyes stray out to the water, where Tommie and Alex sat on their boards like dark seals. Doug was moving slowly up the beach. "Jason, there's something I want to tell you," she said, sounding cautious.

"Yeah?" I asked. I knew it was something about us. I didn't mind being close to Cat. I really liked her, but she often went serious on me at times I was feeling just about good enough to float away. I guessed she could sense when I was feeling high and wanted to capitalize on my good mood. But I can't tell you how much I hated SERI-OUS TALKS. I kept staring away from her, noting that Doug had found a starfish he flung, skipping it out over the waves.

"Jason. How do you feel about what we've been doing?"

"Huh?" I hesitated. My face flushed involuntarily with anger. Why the hell was she bringing that up? As if I alone was at fault for something. Seconds ticked by slowly.

"I'm . . . pregnant." Her voice, a hush.

I caught my breath and then exhaled and inhaled, the air salty and cold. I sat there gloomily. I *wanted* to be close to her, but I knew I wanted, also, to run down the beach and be clear of her forever. I was like a riptide, churning. I thought I was going to shout at her to leave

111

me alone. I thought about just holding her. I didn't do anything but stare out to sea. She sat there awhile. Then she stood up and pulled away the wisps of hair the wind beat about her mouth and face. I thought if she cried, I might smack her, but she just turned and walked up toward the cliffs, her figure dark against the white sand and shrinking.

35. The Show

Doug says Santa Cruz is sometimes referred to as the Coney Island of the West. I suppose that's because it's got this rickety old wooden roller coaster and a boardwalk on the beach. It's been there since the last century. It's really fabulous. It draws lots of tourists, yet is really more of a college town, what with the University of California tucked in the hills surrounding it. The place is party city in summer, in winter, full of students and longtime locals. Senior citizens and kids.

Have you ever noticed that those two groups have a lot in common? Kids and old people travel around in cars in groups all the time. And everybody is always talking about how important they are but nobody seems to have much use for them. They both like to speak their minds and don't care if you like it or not. I'm kind of looking forward to being an old lady. I'll bet I'm a real kook then.

Jason had arranged to leave our things in the Bronco. We'd get them again that night, when we returned to the beach. He led us on a short walk to a heavily traveled street, where we caught a city bus that emptied us near an arcade fronting the boardwalk and all the action. Soon enough we saw where the show was set up in a giant parking lot adjacent to the buildings on the water.

All morning my head was light, empty; the distance between Jason and me seemed pulled hard to splitting. I convinced myself I had surprised him and he was going to take his time getting accustomed to what I had said. But I was down, feeling almost overwhelmed. I told myself it might work out somehow. And yet I'd never seen the coast, and when we finally arrived at the tournament, I couldn't hold on to any of that and oddly felt myself slipping into the quick current of the day. The wind was snapping the colorful flags and banners that were flying. The sun out, air brisk and pleasant. There weren't the crowds we had expected, only a few hundred people at best. We edged up to the front of the spectators and sat on the warm blacktop, front row.

Doug was explaining how there were two main types of competition: half-pipe and street. This would be street competition, which meant, if I understood him and what I saw correctly, that each in-line skater ran a timed course of standard iron rails, wooden ramps, and walls. They received points for the difficulty and smoothness of the tricks they performed while moving over the obstacles.

There were humongous speakers blaring music, and the crowd seemed to be made up of dedicated skaters. Everyone was excited to be there. Jason especially. He kept whipping his head around, taking in every detail as if each thing mattered and had some kind of cosmic meaning. I liked skating, but to Jason it was religion. That's typical of true skaters. It's a life, not a sport, not a hobby.

The course was the length of one half a small city block. It had a launch on one end, a small half-pipe curving into the air on the other. To one side of the middle of the course a wall ramp, on the other an odd elbow-shaped ramp and wall. In the center was a large wooden box with short ramps leading to it from all four angles. Near that were three iron railings, one about a foot off the ground, another about three feet high, and the last one was maybe six feet high with a ramp running to it; the pipe had a kink in it that created a drop to a lower bar. It looked intimidating. Doug said it was standard.

The skaters had already completed their preliminary runs by the time we had arrived, and the crowd was gearing up with enthusiasm for the real show. There were a lot of photographers standing around, sent there by company sponsors, and some other adults officiating and setting up, but the crowd was mostly young, kids twelve to about twenty, I'd guess. There were four pros skating that day: a sixteen-year-old from northern California, an eighteen-year-old from Chicago, one boy in his early twenties from Oklahoma, and one nineteen-year-old from Australia.

We were tuned tight with anticipation by the time the first boy, the skater from Chicago, climbed to the top of the launch ramp, waved to the judges, and dropped, shot with sudden speed onto the pavement. He hit the first box launch hard and lifted off the ground, grabbing the toes of his boots and twisting sideways in an elegant pose before landing. With the swift momentum he'd gained, he twirled backward and hopped onto the short grind rail, sliding over it quickly. He lifted off, knees high, and landed face forward again, dropped to the pavement, and rushed the half-pipe at the other end of the course. There he rose like a skier, somersaulting to land backward, then pivoting sharply and launching up onto the high rail for a spectacular grind along its edge and down the kink in the pipe. Next he pumped with all his might toward the center box, launched, and spun himself in a 360-degree turn before finding the ground on the other side. Finally, he sped into and up the wall ramp to spin above it, then plummeted to nail the ground and roll to the center of the parking lot, where he bowed ceremoniously. It had taken only seconds. The crowd cheered with abandon. Doug and Jason jumped in the air and shouted.

And so it went with equally amazing runs from the others. They each made two full performances for the appreciative crowd, and then it was simply over. Or so we thought, because then the announcer called for anybody there who wanted to try his luck on the course to sign up at a booth posted in the corner of the lot. It was to be an open amateur competition. The crowd buzzed. I looked at Jason. He was looking up at a seagull rowing overhead.

Doug nudged him and said, "Well, hotshot?"

I knew Jason was good. Before he'd moved in with Jackie and me, he'd spent long afternoons behind his house practicing on a half-pipe he and his dad constructed out of plywood. And he was definitely skilled on the streets, doing tricks at every opportunity.

"No skates," Jason said.

I hadn't thought of that, and I felt my heart sink for him, imagining his disappointment as profound, judging by how subdued he seemed—as if to wall off the hurt before it hit him.

"We've got to show them what a Raven can do. *Somebody* here has skates your size. C'mon!" Doug grabbed him by the arm and pulled him into the crowd.

I remained there wondering which would be better for Jason: to be left out of the game or to enter and lose. Behind me I heard a voice say, "Hey, sunshine." I assumed it was Tommie or Alex. I turned to see Barry standing there in a bright banana-colored shirt, chestnut eyes, smiling.

Some spoiled squirt of a kid with a bruised shoulder who couldn't skate for squat had a pair of blades that fit me. He'd come up from Los Angeles with his folks in a Winnebago. Doug and I asked about a hundred people before his mom heard us and offered me his gear.

The guy manning the booth asked, "You have enough experience for this course, son?" I was so stoked I could hardly get out an answer. But yes, I knew what I was doing. Yes, my parent could sign a legal waiver for me. Yes, Barry *was* my legal guardian.

I don't know what we'd have done if Barry hadn't dropped out of the sky to help us. He'd found a poster in my room telling about the exhibition and put things together and driven like mad over to the coast, leaving late that morning. He'd let us know Jackie was pretty unhappy about the whole thing but that he'd leave the mess to her when we got back. He agreed to sign the papers if we agreed to come back without a fight that evening. For myself, I felt relieved we didn't have a long hitch back, anyway. With or without Barry we would have to face the music; heck, why not just enjoy the luxury of an easy trip home?

There were only four kids willing to give the course a go. The judges passed out numbers to us, and we huddled at one end of the course, nervous, waiting. The

118

announcer called out the first entry, the local favorite, a college guy the crowd cheered loudly. He wore a knitted beret and a funky red-and-yellow tie-dyed T-shirt that made him seem, to me, caught in a Deadhead time warp. He was pretty good. He got a lot of big air above the wall and could do these trick fakies—starting out facing forward, then switching to a rear stance midair—with precision. He was a little slow, though, and his footwork seemed clunky.

Next up was a girl. She was only about four feet tall, but she had some muscle and good concentration. She was, oh, maybe sixteen. She wowed everybody with a backflip going over one of the boxes, landing perfectly without so much as a wobble. She was fluid and pretty and had guts. Being small and compact allowed her speed for her flips but robbed her of the weight she needed to get the air time the judges usually looked for.

A kid that had flown out with his dad all the way from Colorado followed her with mostly routine stuff, able but not catchy enough. He lost it grinding the kink rail and smashed his knees up bad enough that he had to quit. I heard, "Fifteen," echo from the speakers. I was up.

I climbed to the top of the launch, and just before I let loose, I saw a kid in the stands that looked like Ishmael, though I knew that was just my head trying to throw me. I heard a scream that sounded like Cat; then I blanked out all sound and jammed. I shot over the box with a 180-degree fakey, landed smoothly, and pumped toward the half-pipe. I took it with all the speed I've ever put together and spun at the top with enough phat air to surprise even me. I knew then I had entered some kind of special zone, that I was untouchable. I came back down the course, taking the ramp up to the high grind rail, and did a series of quick-switch stance hops before greasing the kink without a hitch.

I knew if I could ace the wall, I'd be home free. I came in at an angle, rocketing up the wall like a god in one of those myths Davies was always pushing on us in class. I grabbed my knees and flipped backward, felt my wheels touch down, and knew I was, for that moment, IT. People started cheering wildly. Cat broke from the crowd to hug me, and Barry and Doug appeared, smiling from ear to ear and slapping me on the back so hard I started coughing.

That's how I learned that maybe it's good enough to have everything click just once in your life. That was my day. I was even told by a couple of promoters that I could come back next year and they would give me a shot at the tour. It was pretty heady stuff and seemed, I've got to say, at least right then, worth all the risk we'd taken to get there.

37. The Boardwalk

It was too late to make the drive home that night. No, we were not sleeping on the beach. "Sorry, guys," Barry said, "but I'm not waking up with sand in *my* shorts." And no, we could not sleep out there by ourselves again with Alex and Tommie.

We did drive over to the beach and pick up our things. Alex was still out on his board, catching the last waves of the day, the sun bleeding off into dusk, the water brassy. Tommie unlocked the truck and seemed genuinely disappointed we wouldn't be there that evening. Just before we left, he pressed a crumpled bit of paper into my hand and trotted away, his hair a wild black weed disappearing over the cliff's edge.

I smiled to myself when I unfolded it, glancing at the crooked scrawl. A note scribbled on a candy wrapper in pencil wasn't exactly an invitation to Buckingham Palace, but it was sweet. And a little sad. Reading it, I realized that somewhere along the way I had stopped thinking of other boys.

> Cat,
> If you ever come back, I could teach you to surf. Call me? (415) 555-7645
>
> —Tom

We drove back down to the boardwalk and waited in the car while Barry rented a room at a comfortable economy place called the Lazy Eight Motel. He came back to the car, and we carried our stuff over to the room. The guys watched a boxing match on the telly. Typical. I grabbed the first shower. When I finished, the boys showered. Barry took a short walk to get some smokes and to call Jackie. When he got back, we were all complaining of hunger and imagining what we'd like for dinner.

The motel was only blocks from the boardwalk, so we decided to walk. On the main tourist drag near the water, there were tons of dinner houses. We chose a place called Al's Seafood that had an old rotted dinghy out front filled with ice plants and daisies.

Jason, still high from his triumph, jumped into it and started shouting, "Leeward, lads, the white whale goes that way!" I knew his knowledge wasn't literary—old flicks, late-night telly.

Barry and Doug and I hurried into the restaurant and got into line for a table, pretending no relation. We could see Jason through the windows clambering around in the thing, knock-eyed, trying to look salty and mad. No one must have paid him any mind because he gave up and joined us about the time we got a table.

We gave Barry all the cash we were carrying, counting it out on the table—$17.42 total—and ordered up as much of the Friday fish and chips special as we thought we could eat. It got dark gradually, the lights of the boardwalk spinning excitedly outside the window. By the time we left Al's, the air had cooled, and we put on our jackets.

Barry said he'd treat us to some time on the board-walk if we had the sense not to mention it later to Jackie, so we crossed the street and walked up a big concrete ramp there to the entry. We floated around for a while, soaking up the carnival chaos of lights and bad food and scads of people jostling about.

We decided the roller coaster wasn't to be missed, and we all bought tickets, even Barry. Most of its scare hinged on the fact that it was so old, with wooden tracks creaking and the chain-driven rollers crunching.

As we poised in our buckets at the top of the first rise, Doug and Jason stood up, arms in the air; I hung tight to Barry. Released like a tightly held rubber band, we shot over the course and careened around, screaming our heads off, finally whisking into the tunnel that returned us to the loading dock, panting, our blood up and running.

Next, we did the Ferris wheel, a little slow, but I insisted because it made me think of what they might have on a boardwalk in England. This time I rode with Jason (snuggled in close). He smelled of soap and clean hair. I knew he was feeling proud of himself and generous, because he pulled me to him and laughed. I thought that maybe it was all right between us after all. The lights spun crazily, and I felt as if their light shone inside me, too. After that we rode the bumper cars, Barry begging off because his legs were too long. We were sidewinding around in the little cars that looked like bright ladybugs trying to knock the bloody heck out of one another when I noticed that Barry wasn't standing at the rail any longer.

It struck me as funny because he had been acting very parental and cautious with us as if he knew it was important to Jackie to bring us back unharmed and quickly.

When the ride was over and we were climbing out of the cars, I caught a glimpse of some guys talking to Barry across the boardwalk near the seaside railing. Barry was giving them a big, wide grin, his teeth flashing prettily, but I could tell something was wrong. The boys noticed, too, because Doug elbowed Jason and nodded toward Barry. A foul look crossed over Jason's face, and he called out, "Hey!" as we pushed our way through the throngs of kids and their parents. When we got there, we could see these three guys in their thirties or forties with tractor caps on, beards hanging about their faces like sheaves of tobacco. One of them was shoving Barry.

He wasn't smiling any longer, and his eyes were swinging worryingly from one guy to the next. Jason and Doug and I stood there frozen in some kind of shock. One of the guys, the biggest, took a swing that Barry blocked handily with a sudden thrust of his elbow. That seemed to enrage the three of them because they started kicking at him. I screamed and saw Doug stepping forward in a state of confusion. I saw Jason size up the situation immediately. Jason isn't big, but he's tall enough, quick with his fists and lean and hard. I saw his eyes narrow, a quick smirk cross his lips, and then to my horror, he shrank back into the crowd. Suddenly the big guy, his belly slopping over his belt, rushed Barry, caught him, and lifted him, the other two grabbing ahold, too, and in one seamless and horrible motion cast him over the railing. I saw his arms flail the air, and then he was gone into the darkness. I must've still been screaming because the three of them ran into the crowd that had stopped its milling, vaguely aware something was happening.

Doug and I raced along the boardwalk, found a stairway, and ran onto the dark beach until we found Barry sitting in a slump, his hand covering his head. We knelt in the cold sand. "Barry, are you OK?" I'll admit I was a little hysterical. He was just shaking his head, and his eyes looked glassy. I touched his head, felt the warm surge of blood.

"I guess his boots must of scraped me pretty good." Barry breathed quietly.

"Oh, Barry," I said. "Barry." I knelt to take him in my arms and rocked him slowly to comfort me as much as him, I think.

People were hanging off the rail above us, gawking. Barry looked up at them and said, "Help me up. I just want to go."

"I'm waiting for a cop," said Doug. "We can't let this go."

"Barry, we're going to the hospital."

"No way, pussycat. You're talking to an old bar fighter." He held out his hands, appraising them. "This isn't anything. C'mon, now. Let's get out of here."

Jason appeared out of the dark, looking wide-eyed, pretending innocence. He had this cheesy little half smile, half grimace on his face. "Hey, what happened?" he said tentatively.

I hauled off and hit him, solid, in the chest. He stepped back, saying, "Hey, tiger! Easy! I'm one of the good guys."

"*Damn* you, Jason!" I kicked him in the shin, hard as I could, though not hard enough.

38. Shit

When it happens, I say let it. Next time things go wrong around *you*, notice how people blame everybody but themselves for what's going on. Cat doesn't think anything of hanging all over Barry when he's around, even though she's got enough experience to know it can cause problems. Barry doesn't stop her. And I didn't see Doug jumping in and mixing it up with three fat Bigfoots fresh out of the redwoods.

The upshot was that we walked back to the room and Cat cleaned the cut on Barry's head while he acted nonchalant, like getting slammed was an everyday affair, big deal, etc. Doug and I spent the night on the floor, and Barry crashed by himself in a bed the size of Kansas and went to sleep, solid as marble. Cat curled up in a little Leatherette chair by the window and half cried herself to sleep. For a couple of hours I watched the neon motel sign buzzin' on the ceiling, which is not my idea of excitement. I had to listen to Doug snoring, Cat whimpering, until I let go and slept.

Come morning I crept out and went down to the beach. The gulls were patrolling. A lone brown pelican skimmed the waves, looking for breakfast. It must have seen something because its wings climbed up a little staircase of air, folded, and popped into the surf. If only this were next year, I might make the tour and be quit of all

127

the hassles. I sure as hell didn't want to go back to that motel room any more than I wanted to ever see Whitson again. Or Cat.

But there she was walking toward me, her shadow rippling in front of her across the sand like her only friend. When she got close, I turned my back and picked up a stick and started poking a dead jellyfish the tide had left. She stood next to me. I felt like a scab with her silence picking at me. Finally, I said, "Where's Doug?"

"I suppose he's still asleep," she said in a bitten-down voice. Hurt. Pissed.

A yellow Lab was running by himself along the water, ragged and wet. I whistled to him, but he just slapped on by us, his tongue lolling, smiling, oblivious—happy, I guess.

"You know, Cat, I'm tired of all this." It just rolled out on its own.

She glanced sideways, into my eyes, to see if I meant it.

"I don't know what you expect me to do."

Her face started scrunching up like somebody or something had pulled a thread too tight. I remember thinking she still looked pretty and that maybe that's all there ever was between us—that power her looks gave her. Then she squinted at me, turned, and left. After a while I got tired of all that ocean out there, sliding around, full of itself. The sun came up, hot as ever, making the back of the water shine.

When I got back to the room, Cat and Doug were talking softly, Doug slurping on some coffee out of a little plastic mug. He'd brewed it in the bathroom. Complementary. I was hungry and asked in a full voice if we were going to ever get up and out of there. Cat shot me a look meant to kill. Doug played dumb with a lot of phony interest in his coffee. "Well, are we?" I asked. Cat just glared.

Doug said, more to her than to me, "I think I hang with you two just to see what's next." He shut up when she stabbed him hard with those pissed-off eyes.

"Well?" I said.

Cat told me to hold my horses and went over to Barry and cooed in her best dove voice, asking if he was ready to get up. He didn't budge. She shook his shoulder gently, then harder. I motioned to her to let it go. I could see his wallet plainly enough on the dresser and suggested we just get breakfast and let him sleep. Cat didn't think that would be right and sat down on the floor. Doug walked over and peered down at Barry, his voice thick when he said, "Jason, take a look here."

I crossed to the bed and looked down. Barry's face had gone a weird ash color. I dared a light tap with my fingers to his eyelids, then put my hand over his lips. Nothing I could feel. Doug and I glanced at each other. I thought Doug was going to cry when he said, "Don't tell me he's dead."

39. The Police

By the time the manager and the police and the paramedics arrived Doug was breathing into a paper sack, trying to find reality, his eyes puffed huge with fear. Jason
was hanging back by the bathroom, dulled and guilty. I
couldn't stop shaking. There were about fifteen people in
the room, and it didn't seem like they would stop coming.
The manager kept speaking in Punjabi or something, and
then in the king's English, that he'd never seen us before,
only Barry. The paramedics said he was unconscious, the
cops looking bleary-eyed and bored, except for one of the
detectives, very crisp and curt in his manner.

A woman officer walked me out to the squad cars
where they were parked, snout to snout in the parking
lot. She sat in the backseat with me and held my hand.
She was stocky, her hair coiled tightly in a bun, and I kept
staring at her nails, which were chewed to the quick; she
kept stroking my fingers and asking me if I wanted to tell
her anything. Pretty soon Doug and Jason came out, and
they took us all in separate cars to the station. They
quizzed us mercilessly, asking the same questions, I
learned later. What were we doing there? How did we
know Barry? How did he get that ugly gash on his head?
We told them the truth, and later they pulled us all together and had us describe the three guys on the boardwalk, so they must've believed us. There wasn't much to
tell, since we'd hardly seen them.

They called Jackie and told us she was on her way. I could imagine her, white-faced and speeding toward us like the future, aching to drop a Valium but not doing it because she was driving. We sat in that little room answering questions until I thought I was going to be sick. Barry was in the hospital—in a coma, we were informed. When Jason told them that the guys who attacked Barry did it because he was black, the detective snapped back that was conjecture and to be careful about what we said. Inflammatory stuff wasn't called for and could cause more trouble than we knew. The detective's attitude really made me angry, and I just clammed up. Obviously they weren't really interested in anything but doing the required stuff.

They had a sketch artist work with Doug and Jason on a computer, trying to get the look of the guys. I wasn't interested anymore. Forget them and forget Jason. Doug was too shaken to be angry with. He could still scarcely breathe properly. For a few moments he'd thought that Barry had died there in the room, and it scared him. We were there at the station all day, and when Jackie called to say she wouldn't arrive till dark, they took us to a home for juveniles on a short broken-down block of stucco houses, all with cyclone fences out front and bars on the windows. A couple of counselor types ran the house and mostly let us be to watch television and eat bologna sandwiches and drink a sweet, warm punch they made.

Later, in the early evening, when Jackie did arrive, fresh from the hospital, she was stiff as nails, a checked terror in her eyes. I noticed her lips were carefully etched in deep red. She stood there in the doorway, poised in a tight black dress like one rose balanced, brittle, in a vase, and I thought, What was the use, if all I had been brought into the world was for making her miserable? She wouldn't even look at Jason. I think he was glad of that. Doug was keyed up and seemed relieved to see her. She kept pulling back my hair, and I kept letting it fall forward, my head lowered, as the counselors gave her the rundown. She had a phone conversation with the detective that consisted of a string of twenty or so obedient uh-huhs, and I don't know what on his end. It was past nine o'clock in the evening when we finally sailed out of there in a rented Corolla, onto the coast highway, silent as dust.

40. Silence

I gassed up the rental while Cat and Doug hit the head and Jackie went in and paid, coming back with Cokes and some limp sandwiches in cellophane. Bad sandwiches will always remind me of trouble, I guess. We'd got our share of both that day. It was two in the morning when we pulled into a Texaco in Mojave. I'd been trying to keep my head from rolling off my shoulders for the past hour. I think we should've got a room so Jackie wouldn't have had to drive all day and night nonstop. I guess she knew she wasn't going to get any sleep, anyway, and so why not drive on, clean into the desert?

She hadn't said one damn word, and I think that was worse than if she had really let loose on us. But so far she hadn't. I noticed that a bunch of swallows had built little clay nests that looked like ovens high in the gas station's huge road sign. While they were squeaking and pushing themselves in and out of those dark doorways, I was wishing my life were as simple. Food, a little shelter, flying around. Not bad.

We pulled out and drove on through desert and a bunch of little sleeping towns and then out finally where the land broadened into the valley that was home. Doug perked up and said, "You know, at the turn of the century this valley had enough water for lots of crops until L.A. sucked most of the river into an aqueduct. You see—"

Together Cat and I snapped, *"Shut up."*

He broke off and stared out the window, chin jutting out. I didn't feel sorry for him.

We pulled into town, drove through the quiet streets that seemed smaller and unfamiliar after our being gone. When we pulled into the driveway, Jackie turned off the key and spoke her first words to us, saying, "Doug, you come in and call your parents to come get you. Jason, you can get a little rest. Then you pack your things. You're going home."

part three

41. Remorse

The most difficult thing was that Jackie didn't speak to me for a week. I would see her sitting on the porch in the evenings, her face wrapped in dusk light and smoke—she'd started smoking suddenly—and I would wonder if she was worried for Barry or thinking of what a mess I had turned out to be. The school suspended us for five days for cutting, and I was dreading going back, mostly because I didn't want to see Mr. Davies.

I hadn't had time to miss Barry, though I missed him for Jackie. I think he was under her skin more than she would have ever admitted. I thought I never wanted to see Jason again until a few days had passed, and I knew that was a lie. Sometimes love has a sense of its own. It can be bad and still the only solace you'll ever know. I wondered what was happening with him and his folks.

When I did go back to school, I found that everybody either wanted to know the whole story or had already heard it and looked at me as if I were a leper. Not that I had any real friends except the Ravens, but now I felt spotlighted and embarrassed. Doug came back with a doctor's note saying he could leave class whenever he wanted. He'd get these attacks and couldn't breathe and would go sit in the rest room until he calmed down. I never thought of him as being that sensitive, which only shows you that it takes longer than you think to know somebody.

Jason pretty much acted as if he wanted to forget the whole thing. I knew he tried to stuff things he couldn't handle, but still, it was odd how he seemed to deny that Barry was out cold and strapped down in that little-town hospital like some kind of biology experiment.

He sat with me at lunch, though we didn't speak. I couldn't help smiling a little when he sat down. I know it made him think he could get away with anything, but I never was very accomplished at pretending.

Mr. Davies tried hard to be friendly and told me he was glad I was safe and said he still needed help with Bobbie. But I knew I had disappointed him, even surprised him because he looked at me with a kind of new caution. He told me someday I'd need to talk about it and he would listen if I wanted.

Ozzie was back, full of questions. He thought we were the genuine hole-in-the-wall gang. Silly. He wouldn't be so idiotic if he took a hard look at Doug and me and saw what a mess we were. I was in a kind of shock that made me feel as if what had happened had happened to someone else. When you come that close to genuine trouble, you try to slip away from it as quickly as you can. Karendeep was polite and respectful, though a little distant. More than usual.

Jackie found out that Barry was in a kind of sleep from some kind of aneurysm. A blood vessel had opened a little hole, like a dark flower, in his brain—probably from the beating. He would be here in Whitson, right now, watching television or making a late-night sandwich or sleeping in his own bed if he hadn't come after us.

His sister had to rent a car and go get Barry's beautiful old ride. Barry's sister came by the house with an old woman with white hair and Barry's pecan face who started sobbing softly when she saw Jackie. His mother. I never thought of Barry as having a mother. Jackie went along to see Barry and to drive one of the cars home. They took off together, the three of them looking stunned and forlorn and a little tentative with one another, Jackie perched in the backseat by herself. At least, it didn't rain.

That night the moon rose bright as a new nickel, oblivious and secretive as ever. The wind picked up around two in the morning. I know because I was up and wishing very much that things were different.

Bernard made me laugh. While I was away, he had started fixing up some of his mountains of junk. I guess he got bored without me to spy on. He took a lawn mower and rigged it with electronic gear from a model airplane so he could direct it, remote control, from the front porch. The first time he used it, it took off, jumped the curb, putted across the street, and smashed into the neighbor's Lincoln. He put together a float in the bathtub that would shut the water off when it was done filling. It stuck while he was in the living room reading the paper—flooded the basement!

His masterpiece and one success was an alarm that went off when the mailman opened the mailbox out at the end of the drive. It set off a small air horn he had mounted in the kitchen. The trouble is he showed it to some of the neighbor kids, so it was always going off, all hours of the day and night, and he had to disconnect it.

He tried to get me interested in a notion he had going about wiring the stove so that one of the gas burners would fire up at 6:00 A.M. to heat water for Mom's tea. I told him to buy a good fire extinguisher before he went any further, which only made him look at the ceiling and blink, saying, "OK, OK, you'll see, smart guy."

Mom was busting her butt cooking up all these horrific meals for me. She thought that the cure for all problems were three squares, plus snackolas in the evening. Of course, she rarely ate, and seemed thinner, more hopeless than ever. I think when she finally goes, she'll just dry up like a husk and drift off.

I decided to spend my five days of suspension mapping out a routine to practice for next year's skating tryouts. I wanted something fresh and unusual. With all that talent out there, I figured I needed an edge. I needed something more than the expected thing. I sweated over it the whole time but never settled on anything sure.

I ran into Officer Moxley first day back to the grind. He was leaning on his patrol car across the street from the high school. When I passed, looking him square in the eye, he said, "Hey, bud, guess what I hear. Ishmael's out and looking for you."

I snapped back at him quick and asked him what the hell was he talking about, trying to seem curious but coming off angry, probably.

"Let us know if the police can be of service," he said, wiping his creepy little mustache with his fingers. I shrugged, faking innocence, and walked away. But I'd heard him, and my mind started sputtering, dying, and coughing to life like one of Bernard's useless treasures.

43. Confession

I hung up the phone. Jason again, calling every evening, being very attentive. He sounded lonely. That was the kind of thing that always pulled me back to him.

It was late. Saturday night. Jackie was home, out in the back, doing her new Jackie thing. She was stuck, the way a boat drifts aground, without knowing how big a thing she'd hit on or when she'd get off it or how. I strayed out to the back and stood watching her, etched silver through the metal crosshatching of the screen door. She looked hazy and small, almost invisible in what little moonlight was reflecting back from the sky. For the first time I could imagine her in a few years when I'd be gone, and I wondered if she sensed how fast time was moving.

"Mom, do you ever think of Daddy?"

She stirred as if rowing back to me ever so slowly.

"No. I guess I don't."

She turned her head almost imperceptibly. "Does that disappoint you?"

"No."

" 'Cause we were only close for a short while, kitten."

"Do you think about Abigail?"

"I used to. But I had to put that away."

"What do you mean?"

She thought for a moment. The crickets had warmed up and started playing for keeps. "You know, how you finish a good book? It comes to its end, expected or unexpected. You put it away. You do it carefully. You say, 'This is the end, and now I'll save it.' " Silence.

"Is it crazy for me to think of her? To think I've let her down?" I said, only half conscious of what I was saying.

"I know how that feels." She flicked her cigarette into the grass, where it hissed and darkened, quashed in the dew that had formed.

I knew if I was to ever know, I had to ask now, whether it hurt her or not. "Why did Dad leave?"

"You shouldn't think about this stuff. There's nothing there that can help you." She turned around fully, trying to see me through the door, and answered slowly, "I was sixteen when we got married. Sixteen." This fact seemed to captivate her, and she held on to it for a bit, then continued. "He had to quit school. That was no big deal. He was a guy that liked things simple. He even *wanted* to get married. Have a wife to keep his house. He liked construction. It was different for me. I wanted college, something of my own." She turned away. "Cat, I don't miss him."

"But why did he leave? Leave *us*," I added.

"I don't know. How about that?" She laughed dryly. "Turns out probably the biggest event in my whole damned life, and I don't know. All he ever gave you is that pretty yellow hair of yours, you know. I wouldn't bother my head about him."

I hesitated and then: "If you could go back and change it, would you still have me and Abigail?"

She was only half listening. "No. I guess not," only thinking out loud then. And I knew she just meant she wouldn't choose all the trouble. Still, it stung.

44. Cornered

I was thinking of Moxley, and that pissed me so much I was grinding my skates and slinging my legs with everything I had. Sometimes things get to be too much: Barry smashed up and dopey; Moxley and his quick little Chihuahua face; Bernard, slow, helpless-to-change Bernard; Cat with her moods; and, of course, Ishmael always out there, quiet and sure as a bat about to drop like a hand on my shoulder. So I skated. I took the long blocks that split Whitson with a slow, rising pace, breath huffing like a big dog, my mind slowing down. I rocketed into the underpass at Belmont, skates making a low rumble down there, and shot up onto Divisadero. A smile took over my face, and I started to laugh to myself. I felt good. Strong. Alive.

The weather had warmed some, and earlier Ozzie and I had decided to get some skate time at the park, outside the town's little zoo. He'd discovered some great sidewalk paths that wandered from there to a small amphitheater nearby. He'd said he'd bring John Charles with him. I'd never got around to leaning on J. Charles for spilling the beans about the Davies thing because it didn't seem to matter anymore.

I found them lying on the grass just inside the park entrance and got them off their dead butts to practice getting some speed coming down the theater's wide concrete aisles where we could brake at the lip of the orchestra pit. That John Charles was a certifiable klutz. He swooped down and flew right out and into that hole, a spinning ball, arms and legs flying. He hit with a dull thud and lay there like a cement bag.

"You're supposed to brake, John Charles," Ozzie counseled, peering down at him. J. Charles was hurt, a new bruise spreading on his knee. But it was funny, and Ozzie and I couldn't help laughing. "Did you see how his legs twirled!" Ozzie sputtered.

"Help me up, you guys," John Charles said faintly. Flies were zooming around his head, and he waved them away, sticking out his lip and looking as if he might cry. We helped haul him out of there, brushed him down some, Ozzie lying his head off, telling him he was getting better on skates every day and not to worry.

We were sliding around by the zoo's entrance when I spotted it, the trim white Impala parked in the shade of a huge old monkey puzzle. My heart slammed in my chest. I spun around, scanning the area, and sure enough, there was Ishmael and two of his buddies sitting on a hill of grass a little ways off, watching us. I looked at Ozzie. He was backing away. "It wasn't me. Jason, it was Doug. . . . Doug told him to ask you if he wanted to know anything about Baby Saul."

"You little liar," I growled.

"Honest. I knew he talked to them. I couldn't tell you. You'd blame me." He was still retreating.

I hesitated. I wanted to beat him silly. I could never believe anything Ozzie said.

"Honest, Jason. Why do you think Doug's not here?"

145

That stopped me. I didn't have the time to fool with him, and what he said made sense. I took off, racing toward the zoo's entrance, unable to think of anything else. I left J. Charles and Ozzie standing there, stupid and openmouthed.

The woman at the gate said no skates, and I shucked them as fast as I could, slinging them over my shoulder. I saw Ishmael and his tribe running from the hill straight at me. I ducked in, the woman selling tickets hollering to me something about bare feet. I ran past kids and their mothers, zigzagging around baby strollers and couples all moving, slow motion, through the heat and the animals loafing in the dirt.

I flew by the big cats pacing their cages and entered a place for tropical birds, loud as clowns, huge beaks glistening like somebody had lacquered them black. They picked up on my fear and started fluttering around, beating their wings against the wire ceiling, and screaming. I heard the steel gate clang closed behind me and knew my "friends" were close. I almost panicked when I realized I might've cut myself off. But I found the exit and tore through it, only to find myself stopped by a wide, dugout display circling some rhinos. I took a breath, steeled myself, and high-jumped over the embankment.

45. Leaning

There. I had said it. Mr. Davies made no indication that he heard me, continuing to tease his paintbrush precisely along the window trim. It was the weekend, one of the first really warm days of the year, and we were busy transforming his den from a dull off-white to a smart cantaloupe orange that Bobbie had picked out. He dipped the brush into the center of a can of paint, balanced carefully on his ladder, and pulled it like a wet tongue along the sill. Beads of sweat on his lip.

"Jason?" he asked, his voice faint.

Oh, God, what did he think of me? I regretted that I'd spoken. "Yes," I said.

"Told your mother?" He looked at me then, over the tops of his glasses, the light like a white wasp dancing at the edges of the lenses.

I shook my head, ashamed to speak.

"How . . . how far along are you?"

I didn't understand. I put my brush down and wiped my hands on my T-shirt.

"How long?"

"Oh. Two months," I managed to say. Yes, I was sure; I'd used a home pregnancy test.

He went back to painting. I knew he was turning it over in his mind. A faint tremor had entered his hands. A long moment passed.

"I think you should talk to Nancy—I mean, Mrs. Janson, the school nurse. She's a friend. I can call her if you'd like."

"No. No, please. Not yet. I . . ." My voice flared off into silence.

"Damn!" He'd slipped and smudged paint onto the windowpane. He paused and shot a glance at Bobbie, who was occupied stirring a bucket of paint at the far end of the room, all ears. He went on. "You should talk to your mother."

"I know. It's just that it's a bad time."

A look of displeasure shot across his face that he covered again quickly with a flat look of stone. "Then why tell me?" His words steel.

I bit my lip. I wasn't going to cry. My shoulders began to shake. He put his brush down and swiftly crossed the room to me to fold me into his arms. "Sorry," he said. He smelled of Old Spice and sweat and safety.

"It'll be OK," he said softly, grasping my arms and pushing me back, arm's length, to look me in the eye. "You've got paint all over you." He snapped a handkerchief loose from his pocket and did a pretty fair job of spreading the daubs all over my face. "Well, that'll have to do." We both smiled.

Bobbie sidled up like a pet wanting attention. He touched my face, took a little paint onto his finger, and closed his eyes to draw it with seriousness across his eyelids and brow.

46. Bailing

I slammed the packed dirt pretty hard but jumped up and started moving, not registering the pain I'd feel later. To that rhino I must've been a phantom running across his yard, though he reeled on his heels to line me up in his sights and trot after me. I reached the rear of his home, a wall made of telephone poles rising eight feet or more, chucked my blades over it, and leaped with all I had. My hands shot up as I lifted off the ground, but I couldn't reach the top and slid down to turn, facing the thing that snorted and moved its head sideways to eye me with one huge whale eye. The smell of him, that close and strong, struck me almost as funny for a split second as I backed sidelong across the wall toward a point that I saw dipped lower than the rest. I jumped. A crashing thump shook the stumps below me, but I held on and struggled over and out of there, safe.

I scooped my skates from the ground where they'd landed, thrashed through some bushes, and found a chain-link fence covered with ivy that I hopped to find myself on the street, traffic swishing by in a hurry. I laced up and beat it. When I got home, I went straight to my room, tossed some stuff in a bag, clothes, blanket, matches, a candle. I considered leaving a note, thought better of it: asking for attention I didn't want. No note. I was ghosting down the hall, taking a last glance at Mom and Bernard in the living room sitting like the dead, blue in the pulse from the tube when Mom spotted me.

"Jason?" Her voice cracked. She stood up, all her knitting gear tumbling to the floor, her face pinched. "Jason? Honey? I've got some chicken and coleslaw in the fridge for you." It was more of a plea or an apology than an offer, supposed to make up for Bernard sitting there stupid with liquor, I guess. She was coming toward me, edging past boxes of junk that were always there stacked around the living room.

"All right," I hollered over my shoulder. I was already buzzing down the hall to my room to stash my bag.

She appeared at the door. I turned and shut it most of the way and poked my head out.

"Dear, are you OK?" Her face chipped with concern the way all her porcelain was broken and glued together.

"Yeah, sure, Mom. Hey, could I have that chicken in here?"

"Well . . ." Her face brightened. "Well, of course. I'll—well, I'll just fix you a plate. You can have a picnic." She was all enthused about that. Everything was fine. Son at home. A picnic. It really captured her imagination, which is, I tell you, where she lived.

I threw myself on the bed and switched on the radio, clamped my headphones on, some kind of seventies heavy metal ticking in off the desert. The door edged open. Bernard.

"How's my number one son?" I think he said, his voice a muffled boom, all jolly with false authority.

I nodded.

150

He came in and stood unsteadily, leaning a little on the dresser. A framed photo of me in skate gear slid off its top. He bent to retrieve it, holding on to one of the drawer handles to steady himself so that a tin horse there that I'd won at the fair toppled over.

He didn't notice. He was struggling to get the picture. He was getting down on his knees to fish around. I felt my heart tighten. I looked away. I think he forgot I was there. I could hear him scuffing around down there with difficulty. When I made myself look back, he'd got it and pulled himself up. He placed it back on the dresser top carefully. He brushed it with his fingertips, dusting it, I guess. He stared at it a long while.

I took my headphones off. "Dad, it's OK. Looks good," I said softly.

He turned and looked at me as if I'd just materialized. "How's my number one son?" His voice, quiet now, curious.

"I'm good. Good, Dad." My head nodding.

He started looking right through me, into the wall behind me, I think. "Your mom worries, you understand. Women worry."

"Sure."

He found my eyes again. His eyes, gray with little streaks of blood. "How's the cash flow?"

I shrugged.

He started tugging at the pockets of his shirt. The same white one he went off in every morning, ironed crisp and then always somehow as wrinkled come evening as the topographical maps they showed us when I was in

151

Cub Scouts. He moved his hands to his pants' pockets and started exploring them and came out with a mess of crumpled bills and coins that he placed on the bed. "Take it. Take all you want." He looked shriveled standing there, as if all the air had been sucked out of him. "Go ahead," he urged, his arm sweeping out big, BEING GENEROUS. There was maybe eight bucks, change included. I rolled it into my fist and looked up slowly. Empty doorway. The air went out of me.

Then I got hold of myself, grabbed my bag, and as an afterthought slipped that photo out of its frame and slid it into my bag. I glanced down the hall. He was back in his chair, facing away. Mom was clattering happily in the kitchen. I ducked through the door to the garage and out.

Above me clouds were sliding in, the sky getting dark, a lid shutting down. The first fat raindrops heavy as bees struck my face as I slipped out the back and skated through the alley, free, alone, only the knocking of my skates over rough blacktop.

47. Rain

I heard the soft plosives of rain on the windowpanes. Somerset, Dorset, Devon, and Hampshire—all those pretty English syllables would only exist on a map on the wall now, and I wondered if always the rain would remind me of them. I went to the window to watch the lightning branching in the distance. Porch lights flickered, dark leaves pouring past. I struggled and pushed up the window, letting the smell of the earth that the damp had released sift into the room.

I thought of Jason's face against mine, his breath coming in faint chuffs, his blue eyes, all that rage lighting him from the inside, and then him going soft against me. He was only a boy. I thrust my hand out the window to feel the pinpricks of moisture. A boy who always *ran* from trouble. And the rain eased to a blowing mist, gentle and light, the way my life came to me then, soft, secret after secret.

48. Boxed

I went directly to the Roost. I liked it there because it had the feel of a shadow world. You know, there's a sense something might happen when you're in the dark. Could be that people who had been dead a long time, who once lived there, pulled me to it. I dunno. I had nowhere else to go till I figured things out. I'll admit when I got there and settled into the front bedroom upstairs, rolling my blanket out and lighting my candle, I wasn't feeling very free. The rain hadn't been much, and I was still fairly dry. I ate an egg salad sandwich I'd bought at the 7-Eleven, spent some time thinking about how I'd like some water or a Coke, and then I was out of things to do. I wished I'd brought some magazines and a flashlight. Then I heard a crash downstairs and the faint sound of cursing.

I flashed to the window. No car in the street, just the rain, fine in the streetlamps. I started groping around the room for something I could swing in case I needed it. All I could find was a wooden hanger. That wasn't going to do any damage. I'd already changed into my tennis shoes and so grabbed one of my skates from the floor and snuffed the candle. Pretty soon I heard some shuffling outside the door. I crept into the closet and pulled the door nearly shut and peered out.

Into the gloom came a figure. It moved to the center of the room and sat down heavily on the springs of that

154

old bed, which squeaked noisily. Whoever it was was
looking around. Spotted the candle. A match flared.
Touched the wick and let it flame. It was a man, glistening, wet. I could tell he was only mid-thirties or so,
though roughed up and looking worse for every minute
he ever lived. His face looked like it had been hacked
with a blunt ax from a red and white loaf of cheese,
pocked as it was with acne scars. Eyes—black sockets
reflecting the candle, guttering. If they'd had a sound,
they'd have hissed.

He fingered my blanket knowingly, pulling it toward
him, then picked up the skate I'd left on the floor. He
twirled it in front of him, holding it by one of its straps.
"This yours?" He swung suddenly toward where I was
peeking out at him. I fell back with a thud, shot up, and
kicked the door wide.

"Damn straight it is." I snapped off each word.

"Easy, killer." He held his hand up like a cop stopping
traffic. "Might as well be friendly. Looks like we're
roomies, though no reason to get you an extra key seeing
as you've already smashed this door open for good." That
amused him, because he started burping a laugh that
nearly chocked him.

I came out of the closet and stood watching him, still
thinking I might beat it past him and out of there. But to
where? I thought him too decrepit to give me or anybody
else much of a fight. I calmed down some and said, "You
sick or something?" Sarcasm.

He shot me a look that showed he could still be a
force I'd better be careful with, then softened up and said,

"Maybe so. Maybe I am." He was toweling his hair with my blanket.

"What are you sick with?" I was feeling a little dangerous myself.

"The second worst affliction known to man," he announced. "Very fond of wine, my friend. It's a taste I developed early and have practiced long." He was enjoying the sound of his voice. "What's your excuse?" His eyes were sizing me up. "Skater dude," he finished.

"I'm hiding out."

He started sputtering again and waving me off as if I were killing him with humor. "OK. Jesse friggin' J-J-James," he stuttered.

I was getting angry. Who did this cracked-up, dead-end creep think he was, anyway? I switched the subject. "What's the first?" I said, noticing my voice had taken on a false gravel, as if trying to match his.

"First what?" He blinked. "Say, you got anything to sip?"

"No. First affliction."

"That'd be women. Don't you dudes smoke a little dope once in a while?" he said hopefullike.

"No. We *dudes* don't. Least, I don't. Why do you say they're afflictions?" I surprised myself that I thought he might know something I didn't.

"They're the thorn that pestered St. Paul. You kids never read anything, do ya? Heard of Eve? There was that little matter of the apple, you know. Rotten. De-fi-ni-tive-ly rotten." He clucked his tongue once. He thought he was brilliant.

156

"So what?"

He looked at me, taking his time. Pulled a little bag from his shirt pocket and rolled a cigarette handily, fingers a dull yellow, hands scarred from something sharp. "You got a girl? Yeah, I see you do."

I didn't know what to make of that. He enjoyed seeing I was startled.

"Women are the lost half of you. That's why you keep after them, even though they're such a hassle." He drew on his smoke, a little pleasure he obviously enjoyed.

"Who the hell are you?" I asked.

"Name's Horace." Then he threw back his head and laughed like some kind of mad peacock.

49. Loss

I stirred in my bed, my legs swimming, heavy in the sheets. I tried to remember what I had been dreaming, something about a fish, a slow zeppelin, tiny fins whirring, its lips nuzzling salt from my thigh; it lifted and floated away. Then I felt Jason's fist, thrust deep in my belly, as if trying to take something from me. I pushed him away and lifted my legs like thick limbs of deadwood kindling and placed them on the floor and stood, wavering by the bed, looking down at my still sleeping figure— face bleached in moonlight, eyes behind closed lids tracing back and forth furiously. Then I woke. Sharp pain. The sheets wet and dark, sticky as honey.

50. Advice

"No, no, it's over here," Horace said. He was wobbling in the flicker of the candle he held in his hands. The rain had stopped, and we were out back of the old mansion near the garage that Horace insisted on calling a stable. He remembered it as a kid, before the place had been re-modeled, when it still had stalls, though no horses, only rusting gear and an old Model A the old witch—he called her the old witch with some kind of mysterious satisfaction—who still owned the place back then kept around for old times' sake.

We were at the rear of it, where the property line was, marked not by a fence but some old privets and roses that were overgrowing themselves. He was pointing to a leaking spigot that was hidden in grass, two feet high and thick with mosquitoes. We'd gotten thirsty, and Horace was showing me the luxuries of the place as if he owned it. We sucked our fill from the spout, and Horace sank on the wet grass and flung his arms out. I sat down cautiously, wishing I didn't have any company and wondering what the heck was next. The ground was chilled, the wind still up.

"Ahhh, look what the wind blew in. Stars!" he proclaimed. "Boy, in Manitoba, that's where I worked last, mechanic for a big wheat outfit up there. Well, it'll look, on a clear night, one of those cold, still ones, like God or the devil spilled a trainload of salt."

I'd seen my share of stars and wasn't impressed. Too far away to be of any use to me. I was more afraid that somebody would see or hear us, though it was a big lot and not a neighborhood where folks went poking around if they heard trouble.

"So what are you doing slinking around Whitson for, Horace?" What the heck, I might as well satisfy my curiosity, as I wasn't going to get any sleep.

"Got canned. Mean sucker for a foreman up there. I came down on a bus far as Nebraska, hitched out to Utah, and worked a ranch there, welding farm equipment and stuff. Got in a fight with my landlord and took off again in February. Like I told you, I grew up here. Money was gone, and I remembered this old place. You know we used to sneak around in the stable back then the way you guys have taken over the house now." He paused to spit with considerable skill into the bushes. "The old witch, she was deaf and in her nineties. She lived up in that room in the front. After the house went to hell, she just lived in that one room. They carted her off one day, and her son or somebody broke it up into apartments."

Horace must have spent a lot of time by himself because he was rattling on, nothing holding him back, when he stopped suddenly to eye me wickedly, one eye a cue ball, the other, half-mast. "Jesse, what are *you* doing skulking around?"

"Well." It was none of his business, but then again, who cared? "Somebody's after me," I stated simply, almost gloating.

He paused, then: "Well, son, I guess I can say the same."

"Who's after you?" I imagined then what his crimes might be. Murder? He'd said he'd had a fight with his landlord. No, probably theft. Petty theft if I was any judge of character.

"Guy by the name of Horace Anderson."

Now I knew he was crazy. I looked at his eyes. Sparks in the grass.

He yawned. "Fear's a powerful thing if you don't face it. Maybe I've been running from myself, though I can't say why. Just always feel a place, usually some room I'm staying in, start to crowd me, or some woman starts sinking her claws into me and I go. Jesse, I just *go*."

"If you call me that again, I'm going to belt you," I said. He didn't speak. I looked over, staring hard into the dark. He was asleep. An ol' boar, old too soon from living in the weeds. Tusks of hair. Mouth open, just begging for an apple. I slipped the candle from his hand. I was going back inside and needed it.

51. The Call

"Oh, I *do* understand, but I can't help wishing you had told me, pumpkin." Jackie's face was drawn with fear. It was ten o'clock on Sunday morning, some girls from the neighborhood playing tag on the lawn, their voices rising like small bells to my window. Jackie was sitting on the foot of my bed, picking at the fuzz on my blanket. She shook her head slowly. "You're going to be OK. I called Dr. Wilson. He says I'm to bring you to the office first thing tomorrow, even if you're still feeling well." She looked at me closely with new, inquisitive eyes. "Cathy, I've never . . . miscarried. Was it . . . painful?"

"Some, I guess." I struggled to sound offhand. "Mom. Thanks—for not getting angry," I said, though I felt pretty sure once she got over being relieved and started to think about things she *would* be angry.

But right then she was staring out the window. Spring was almost done sawing up the warm yellow days, getting ready for the true heat of summer. The cedar waxwings that always arrived on their long migration north to feed on the berries in our yard had already abandoned the trees in gusts like blown leaves. It would've been a day I'd have spent in bed without what had happened. I sat there in a strange, deep calm, watching Jackie watch the empty trees. Barry was better. He'd awakened one day like a hungover sailor and started cursing the nurses, inexplicably.

His speech had remained slurred, and when I'd listened to Jackie with him on the phone, I could tell she had trouble understanding him because she was extra polite and tried not to give it away when she asked him to repeat things.

She'd told me she felt terrible about what had happened but that she didn't think she could stay with a man out of pity. "It was a *fling*," she'd say. Fling—such a light word for the heaviness in her eyes.

"How about a grilled cheese?" Jackie said, pulling herself out of reverie and slapping the blankets, trying to be cheerful.

"OK, Mom." It felt good to be calling her that again.

She smiled weakly and said, sort of musing to herself, "You won't always be this lucky, you know." Then she turned and went downstairs. That made me think.

I heard her pulling stuff out of the cupboards and humming, a thread of worry in her voice. Yet for the moment my needing her seemed to break her loose from her trouble.

She called up to me, "Cat, I'm going to have to run over to the market. No bread. You be OK?"

"Yes," I shouted. "I'm perfectly fine." Wasn't I?

"Back in a flash."

She'd have to walk, since there were no buses on Sunday, so I knew I had a half hour or more to myself. I got up and went to my dresser to look at myself. I could see no change where so clearly one had taken place. I thought of how a sandbar on the river that gets washed away with the spring water isn't missed unless it was a place you'd noted each day. But there was no change I could find in the mirror until my eyes started welling up and drowning themselves. For the first time I saw, truly, that I was pretty, and it struck me as sad that it was only then that I could see it. I had suspected I was from the way boys always grew quiet around me, but that day I knew it. I wondered then if I would ever have a girl of my own and if she'd be pretty. I felt ashamed and sat down and cried to myself.

The phone jangled me to my senses. I wiped my face and moved carefully down the stairs. I felt all right. I'd survive. Yes, I told myself, I would. I picked up the receiver.

"Hello," I said, almost breathless.

It was Mr. Davies. His voice sounded the way it did in class. Formal, sure. "Catherine, I'm sorry to bother you, but there's a little problem on this end. Bobbie's missing. Catherine, you there?"

"Yes, yes. Missing?" I knew that was one of Mr. Davies's big worries, that Bobbie would stray and put himself in danger.

"We went fishing yesterday. His gear's gone. I went down along the water, but I didn't see him. Catherine, I've called the police, and I'm going back, but there's an awful lot of shoreline. I was wondering if you could get some of your friends and go on down there and look around."

I could tell he didn't want to ask, but I also knew how much he cared for Bobbie. "Sure, sure. Don't worry, Mr. Davies, we'll find him."

"Oh, I know that. He's probably over on the next block or something talking to a neighbor. I'll take another spin through the neighborhood before I take the van down there. I can't tell you how much I appreciate this." He hung up abruptly, betraying how flustered he was.

I dialed Doug. He didn't seem to grasp the seriousness of the situation but said OK, he'd meet me out there on the beach. I told him to bring his skates. There were miles of bike paths skirting the river, and we could move quickly that way, yet be close enough to the water to see anything, if there was anything there to be seen. Next, I buzzed Ozzie. He was confused for a while, but he eventually understood the situation and said he'd get John Charles and to count on them. He reminded me he still was supposed to stay home—house arrest—but he didn't care. He was coming.

Last, I rang Jason. Jason's mother came on and told me how Jason had left suddenly last night and hadn't come home. I got off as quickly as I could, which wasn't very fast at all, because she wanted to quiz me, wondering if I knew where he could be. I more or less convinced her that Jason could be anywhere, though probably on his way home right now. I hung up, raced upstairs, grabbed my skates, threw on a T-shirt and shorts, and bolted downstairs and out of there. I felt suddenly light-headed and remembered Jackie. But I couldn't wait or spend any time convincing her I was well enough to go, so I bolted out the door, pausing just long enough on the porch to snap on my skates. I certainly knew where Jason had to be. A woman possessed, I strode rapidly into the street and pushed the few short blocks I needed to go.

I remember that my body moved smoothly as if it knew it must be purposeful and certain with no energy wasted. I left my skates on when I climbed the broken stairs to the back porch of the Roost. The door swung open easily this time as I entered the ancient burned-out kitchen and called out. Nothing. I skated into the living room and to the bottom of the stairs, making plenty of racket.

Jason appeared at the top of the staircase, wrapped in a blanket, barefoot, hair spiked with sleep. He smiled. "Hey, Cat."

"Jason, Bobbie's missing, and the Ravens are all down at the river looking for him." My words came tumbling and urgent.

He sat down on the top step, his movement slow and thoughtful. "Little man gone fishing by himself, huh?"

"That's what Mr. Davies thinks. He can't swim," I added, urgently.

At that Jason looked at me sidelong, a half smile curling his lip. He seemed edgy.

"Jason?"

"I'm through with the Ravens."

"Jason, we need you now."

"I'm out. In fact, I'm leaving this whole sorry town."

He might as well have slapped me. I was stunned. I thought for a moment, then said what I had to say, evenly and with care, each word measured and sure, "Jason, if you do not come now, I can't be with you anymore. Ever." I meant it.

He looked off across the rooms, huge and listening. "Well . . . I'm getting out of here." His eyes drifted back to me; his shoulders were slumped, his face lean and empty. "I just don't have anything to give you, Cat." He looked sad.

"You could love me." His face was smooth, and his eyes looked watery, like Bernard's, I thought.

"Cat?"

"What?"

"Nothing."

"I have to go."

He nodded. "Cat, you got any money?"

"No."

"Sorry, just thought I'd better ask." He looked at me curiously as if I were new to him, a stranger.

I felt like crying but didn't, the way you do when something has pierced you so sharply you can't do anything but feel your whole body cringing and dying, yet I was still there and alive and found myself watching the sun, how it was round in the window behind his head like a halo moving slowly away.

I sat there for a while, checking myself, like a guy who's looking for his wallet or something, seeing if I felt any different now that I had finally done it. Made the break with Whitson and everyone in it. I couldn't feel anything. Except hungry. I went on upstairs and found Horace's knapsack and rifled through it. Dirty shirts, some cutoffs, a wallet—dry as a dead leaf—expired driver's license, a punched bus ticket, and two soggy five-dollar bills. I snagged them and a box of kitchen matches I found at the bottom of the pack.

I'd wanted to stay on for another night or two and hit up Karendeep for whatever money he might give me, but I couldn't stomach another night with ol' Horace. I stuffed my things along with my skates in my bag. Maybe I could go by the market and Karendeep would give me some chow. Then I remembered, he'd be down at the river. I felt a pang of envy for a second and then shrugged it off and went downstairs. I heard the front door swinging open and froze. I was only halfway down the old staircase and couldn't see anything but the ceiling. "Cat?"

I stretched my neck down as far as I could to get a look. Into my line of sight stepped Ishmael, looking up, neck craned like a mirror image. "Gotcha."

He smiled.

53. The Search

We met up at the beach at the end of Peach Avenue where it failed gradually in the grass and a paved bicycle lane began. All the guys were already there, sitting in the sand, skimming rocks across the water. The river was swollen and running fast and angry. The sudden warmth had triggered the snowmelt.

We were so near the water Karendeep had to half shout to be heard. "Mr. Davies has already been here," he said.

Doug put his hand on my shoulder, "He asked us to cover this side of the river. He went upstream to cross at Stinson's bridge. He's going to take the dirt road as far as it goes on that side."

"I suppose it makes sense to go downstream first?" Karendeep said. He was standing close to Doug, and they both wore looks of doubt and concern. Ozzie was behind them with his arm around John Charles, very fatherly. They were all ears and willing. Looking at those guys, I felt proud of them. And grateful.

"Well, it's logical that it's easier walking downstream, but he could have easily wandered the other way."

"Karendeep, will you take Ozzie and go downstream?"

"Sure, Cat. C'mon, Oz." He was great. No questions—he just went. Ozzie let go of John Charles and started to open his mouth to object when Karendeep grabbed him by the elbow and led him off.

Doug was staring after them. "Come on," I said. And so we began. John Charles trailed us, laboring to keep up. I knew well enough that Ozzie liked to keep John Charles in tow, but I felt if he was going to be near the water, I'd better keep him with me. He followed, without complaint. The water was muddy, yellow with silt, dead limbs, and twigs. Running the banks were a mishmash of cattails and bulrush. Some cottonwoods, sycamore, small drifts of lupine booting the oaks. Any other day it would have been pretty.

We made good time skating with will and scanning the bushes and the water. It didn't take us long to cover a couple of miles or more. I stopped, and Doug stopped, John Charles pulling in beside us. We all were panting, and I labored to shout above the water. "I don't think Bobbie would come this far, do you?" I said.

"I don't know him. If he's like a kid, though, well then, sure, why not?" Doug said.

"If he fell in, he could be way downstream, the other way," John Charles ventured.

Doug and I looked at each other. We knew he could be right. "OK, if that happened, Karendeep and Ozzie will find him. If he's in the trees on the other side where the road goes, Mr. Davies will probably spot him. Let's go up a little further, and then we'll turn back." I said.

They nodded, and we took off. We skated another half mile to where the river narrows and rounds a wall of rock too hard for it to have chiseled through over the years. Once it turned its corner, the water widened and slowed. Suddenly John Charles was shouting. We spun around and skated back to him. He was pointing at the bank where a fishing rod lay and a blue Hawaiian shirt flagged the leafy limbs of a willow. We scanned the river, bright coins of light shimmering on its back. No Bobbie.

We removed our skates and edged down to the water, holding on to branches for balance. When we were close enough to touch water, Doug tapped me excitedly and pointed. There, where the water back-eddied in the shadows of a low-slung cliff, on the far side in a deep, heavy pool, clinging to the branches of a dead tree, was Bobbie, fish-eyed with terror, blind without his glasses, lowing like a lost calf.

54. Caught

Ishmael, like me, was fifteen, going on twenty-two. He had long black hair and the keen, bold eyes of a panther, his face, his skin, a fine red sandpaper. I'd wrestled him maybe a thousand times as a kid and never once pinned him. He was slight of build, which hid his strength and speed. Like me, he had a temper. He had on baggy pants and an over-sized, untucked blue work shirt buttoned at the collar.

Right then he was creeping toward the bottom of the stairs. "Hey, homes, you a hard guy to get hold of," he called.

I said nothing, fast-forwarding my options like sports clips in my head. Leap down the stairs and knock him over? Stand my ground and let him come to me? Take off through the upstairs and see if I could barricade myself in somewhere?

"I'm going to talk to you, that's all. I'm here by my-self. Relax."

He sounded like he was telling the truth, the Ishmael I'd known in elementary school. But what about all the stories I'd heard since then? Weren't they true? For sure, he'd knocked out the top row of Micky Barringer's teeth just for talking to his girl. Some said he strapped a gun to his ankle, but that could be bull.

"Come on. I'm tired of chasing you all over the place. I just wanna know if you know anything about what happened to my little brother." He paused. "I think you do. Doug says you do."

At that I bolted. I tore down the second-story hallway, through a little curved doorway and into what must have been a separate apartment at the back of the building. No doors. A bank of windows facing the back. I pushed one open. It swung out reluctantly, like a small cupboard made of wood and glass. About fifteen feet to my left, I saw a slope of roof angling down over the driveway. If I could get to it, I could jump safely to the ground. Getting there meant sprouting wings and flying or doing some delicate footwork. I slipped out, getting a toehold on an edge of wood facing that ran the length of the house. With my hands I clung to the sills of the windows, now over my head, and I worked down about halfway, popping sweat.

Ishmael's head appeared at the first window. "You're crazy," he whispered, though it sounded like a hiss. I realized I'd made a mistake. He could easily move along the row of windows and open one of them to knock my hands loose. I should have used the last of the windows, not the first, but my mind had been jammed with fear. I glanced at him. I was in trouble; my toes were crammed too tight and starting to cramp.

"You're stuck," said Ishmael.

Didn't I know it! "Look, give me a hand," I panted. What choice did I have?

"Sure. You tell me about my brother."

"Jeez, Ishmael, give me your hand." Sweat was burning my eyes, and my heart was kicking like a horse.

"You were there." His voice, certain and heavy, dropped down to me.

"Yes, for chrissake, I was there. It was an accident. An *accident*."

"You just left him there."

"There was nothing I could do for him. I was going too fast when I hit him. He hit his head. That was it!" I was shouting, panicked and desperate. "Ishmael, if you let me fall, it isn't an accident!" I tried glancing up to see him but couldn't, my eyes tearing.

Then, suddenly, I heard the middle window crack open and felt his fingers struggling to grip my wrist when with no warning, the wooden facing gave way and my right leg slipped. I could feel myself going, so I let loose and made a leap toward the overhang. One leg made it and drove through rotted shingles, caught me firmly in the roofing and snapped me backward, my other leg swinging free. I heard a snap like knuckles cracking in my back, in my hip, down along the one suddenly dead, snagged leg. I hung there, for a second part of the air more than anything else. Then it was like my mind was a city with its lights going down, dark.

55. Fear

It clutched my throat like a cold hand. Doug was stripping down to his shorts, John Charles jumping in little circles, crying, "Oh, damn, oh, damn, damn!" My eyes went to Bobbie. He didn't see us and looked panicked and tired. If we waited for help, somebody to get a boat and try to maneuver out to him, we knew he'd be gone, swept away by the certain pull of the river. Doug sat down as if a large and unseen hand had pushed him. "Doug!" I screamed. His shoulders were pumping, and I could tell he was having one of his fits. I crouched down next to him. "Doug?"

He shook his head. Eyes glossy as a fly's. I looked at John Charles. Useless. I hesitated only a moment, the world spinning around me in flashes: the dirty river, the hot sky, the trees blazing green. I tore off my skates, then my top, tossing it to John Charles, who caught it and stared at me, speechless. At least he'd stopped his foolish screaming. I ran up the beach about fifty yards and waded in, the water immediately deep and icy. I dived.

I swam, trying for a direct line to the other bank, knowing the current, though slowed there, would angle me out, maybe to Bobbie. It was stronger than it looked and was tugging me surely into its flow. In seconds I shot by Bobbie's tree. It was easier pulling back toward the shore I'd come from. My arms slapped the water, and I

175

managed to beach myself on the shore a couple of hundred yards below where I'd left Doug and John Charles and far past Bobbie.

I stalked my way back upstream, crashing through the reeds. I reached the guys, winded, scared, and yelled in brief bursts to Doug and John Charles that I thought I could make it out to Bobbie if I started my entry even farther up the river, where it narrowed. I told John Charles to hustle back down the road with instructions to get somebody down there with a boat, fast as they could. Doug would stay put to mark the spot and to watch me and be whatever help that he could.

"Cat, I'm fresh, and you're beat. I'll go." He was calmer now, but his eyes still looked unsure.

I don't know what I looked like there, half naked and shivering, but I *knew* I was going back. "I'm going." I felt then I could will Bobbie back to shore if I had to. I snapped my skates on and flew out of there.

The path rose sharply to the point where the ground was rock and made a short throat of the river. The water was swifter there, but I planned to dive from the edge and launch myself out farther than before. I picked my spot, a jutting ledge of black rock, moss-covered and slick. I clambered out onto the rock. I stood there for a full minute or more, getting my wind. I was weak, my legs syrupy.

Downstream I could see Doug standing on the shore, waving Bobbie's blue shirt, Bobbie humped like a pale mass of gum snagged in the gray tree midstream. I noticed the side of red barn on the rise behind them seemed

176

oddly poised like one wing of a huge monarch, just landed, and for a second, I thought of Barry, then Abigail. I hoped it wasn't a sign. Then I went.

I arced out as far as I could, didn't feel the cold this time, only the fast sweep of current. It was all I could do to keep my head out of the water. I rolled through the narrow and felt the water loosen its grip some and swam with all I had toward the center, moving downstream by long surges for each stroke I made toward the center. Then there was the tree—Bobbie, face contorted, eyes like burnt cinders. I realized I had no power to make my body intersect with that tree until an eddy swept me toward it, almost too quickly. I ducked a branch and came up and grabbed another and swung myself up, squirming to perch precariously atop it.

Bobbie was turning toward me, and suddenly I knew if he tried to come to me, he'd be swept away. "No. Stay, stay," I shouted. He held fast.

I began working my way along the branch and tried to settle in behind him. He started to reach around to grab me in panic but slipped, and that scared him and he held on again to the branch with a death grip. I put my arms around him and leaned my full weight against him, pressing him to the limb. And that's how we stayed, wed like a couple of insects for a full half hour or more until the sheriff and two volunteer firemen arrived in an aluminum boat to pluck us to safety.

56. Epilogue

Never did see Horace again. I dunno . . . it's like he was part of a dream I had or something, only there for a moment, you know the way a dream might give you a warning that you can't quite make out and so forget. But I think of him once in a while and wonder where he went. He makes me think maybe all of us go careening around, sparking off one another, never really knowing what we've set into motion or why.

Could be some lives are all chance. I guess Horace had his. Chance, that is, like me, but didn't see it. Didn't have whatever it is inside some folks that lets them reach out for what matters. People hate a guy like that. But it's not right because it seems too much a trick that some people have that in them and others don't. So I don't buy into all the drivel about acceptance that people were always serving up to me after the accident as if it was my fault all that happened.

That day Ishmael got the paramedics, and they laddered up and unhinged me. Must have been a show: me hanging by my foot like a dead twig, dangling, out cold. Word was that Ishmael figured I got what I deserved. I know he never bothered me again. I do think of Baby Saul once in a while, but I can't see any profit in feeling bad about it all the time.

I started working on my high school equivalency test,

home studies, and that's when I began thinking of learning by mail how to fix computers. In summer Bernard got sick and lay in the back bedroom being heroic, which in his case meant silent. Drunk. Jowls drooping in folds. He died in September. When they put him in the ground and tossed dirt in after like a hard rain thudding that box, I choked up and almost started crying, but I think it was for myself.

I use his old workbench out there in the garage to repair stuff, though I can't really make a go of it. People want to drop their gear downtown at a shop. I guess they think if some busted-up guy is working out of his home, he must not be very good. Which isn't true, you know.

My leg was splintered, bad, and the nerve damaged. It took two surgeries to leave me with a leg that's two and a half inches shorter than the other and as numb as a tooth shot full of novocaine. It's braced from the knee down so I can swing it from the hip and plant it steadily enough to bring the good leg around, knee bent and looking like I'm climbing a little stair that isn't there, again and again.

Cat and the rest of them were all heroes, and I didn't hold a grudge about that. She got prettier all the time. I found out she lost that kid and that's too bad, I suppose, but I won't say we were right for each other.

Maybe things just go as they go, not because they're supposed to go any particular way in the first place, though that's believing in nothing, which is about the same as believing in something. Takes faith. You decide.

Barry was OK after a while. He came back and played sax as usual, though he got a steady job with the power

179

company entering numbers. I heard you can understand him when he talks if you're around him enough, which I'm not.

I got a basketball, a slick, expensive Wilson, to shoot hoop in the driveway. I can make clean swishes about 90 percent of the time from the top of the key I chalked out on the cement. I pay the little squirts in the neighborhood a buck an hour to shag the ball for me. I guess there's worse things than being strapped in your own body, though all the time I'd like to get out of this place. It's strange how it gets here in October, when there's wind in the trees, and the leaves go a red and black, coming down like burnt feathers. Evenings in the desert can be tricky, sneaking up on you, purple and dark. Sometimes there's gulls, winging high overhead, but they're too high to shoot.

57. Epilogue

Eventually Barry came home, and Jackie and he started up again, very slowly. Together they seemed suddenly old, moving about each other like careful friends, the way married people seem to me to carry some invisible third thing between them, something no longer quite right, yet too good to put down.

I finished my year at school and spent the summer helping with Bobbie. Mr. Davies was right: There did come a time when I had to talk the whole thing out, and he did listen when it all rushed forth, sometimes hot and tearful, but mostly slow and precise as if I needed to hammer each word thin and true so as to leave it and go on, sure that the telling had made it all into a shape, final and needed.

Later he helped me into a student exchange program. I could hardly believe it. I think, now, I did it as much for Abigail as for myself, going to England, a year of study, time to take long, purposeless walks of a kind I'll always miss. Once, in a park in London, I watched a paramedic, a Jamaican girl, sweet in her twenties, try to blow the wind back into the chilled, doll-like face of a tramp who'd drowned so surely dead even the crowd fell away to leave them there, alone like lovers, and I knew what it was that made her go on struggling there on the grass—it's hard to give up on life. It *should* be hard—perhaps that's why I

181

went on loving that way, too long, those who could not love me back: Jason, and the father I've never known.

Yet, there are those that will arrive in your life with the same common majesty of birds dropping to the ground to feed any day in winter. And they can save you. Mr. Davies was that to me, and in a way Barry, too. Perhaps they only pointed the way, and I saved myself.

At times I will remember how new it felt to be alive then, and I see myself, sitting there on the back stoop, watching a dusk sky wobble toward nightfall, thinking of Abigail, looking up at a red kite snagged in the power lines. Just waiting for wind.